HAT TRICK

W.C. Mack

Cover by
Paul Perreault

Scholastic Canada Ltd.
Toronto New York London Auckland Sydney
Mexico City New Delhi Hong Kong Buenos Aires

Scholastic Canada Ltd.

604 King Street West, Toronto, Ontario M5V 1E1, Canada

Scholastic Inc.

557 Broadway, New York, NY 10012, USA

Scholastic Australia Pty Limited

PO Box 579, Gosford, NSW 2250, Australia

Scholastic New Zealand Limited

Private Bag 94407, Botany, Manukau 2163, New Zealand

Scholastic Children's Books

Euston House, 24 Eversholt Street, London NW1 1DB, UK

Library and Archives Canada Cataloguing in Publication

Mack, Winnie, 1972-

      Hat trick / W.C. Mack.

ISBN 978-1-4431-0201-8

      I. Title.

PS8625.A24H38 2010   jC813'.6   C2010-901938-5

  6 5 4 3 2 1   Printed in Canada 121   10 11 12 13 14

Chapter One

The blast of my brand-new alarm clock sounded ten times louder than the lunch bell at school. In fact, I was pretty sure it could be heard from one end of Cutter Bay to the other, and probably from every other town on Vancouver Island.

I imagined the goalie from the Esquimalt Eagles squinting in the dark and wondering what the racket was. And I could practically see the whole starting lineup for the Sooke Seagulls (who smoked us twice last season) scowling and pulling their blankets over their heads.

Nobody loves the scream of an alarm clock at five in the morning, not even the most diehard players in the island league.

I groaned and reached out from under the warmest, coziest blankets on earth and turned it off, ready to sink back to sleep. But I'd barely closed my eyes when Mum knocked on my door. It wasn't a gentle tap with the knuckles, but more of a quick, powerful bang of her fist.

She meant business.

"Are you up?"

"Uh-huh," I grunted, opening one eye.

All I saw was pitch darkness, all I heard was rain splattering against my window, and all I knew was that the wood floor of my bedroom was going to be as cold as the arctic ice floes we'd been studying in Mr. Marshall's class. Probably colder.

My gut instinct was to huddle under the blankets for just five more minutes. Mum knew it, so she banged on the door again.

"You can't be late on the first day, hon."

My eyes popped open as I realized she wasn't talking about school. It was something much, much better than that.

Finally.

The first day of practice!

I smiled in the darkness, picturing the Zamboni slowly circling the rink, leaving a slick, shiny trail I couldn't wait to carve up with my skates. The image was what Dad would call "a kick in the pants," but the good kind. The kind that made me throw off the covers and leap out of bed, excited and ready to go.

I showered and dressed as fast as I could, smiling the whole time. When I met Mum in the kitchen, I was ready for action in warm track pants and my favourite Canucks hoodie (the one with the old-school logo).

"Have you got your gear ready?" Mum asked, buttoning her raincoat.

I nodded. It was my responsibility to keep my equipment organized. Before I went to bed the night before, I'd packed my pads, uniform and all the stuff I'd need after practice for school.

I may not have grown much taller over the summer, but my feet were a full size bigger than last year, so I'd also packed the sweet new Bauers I'd been dying to break in.

Mum handed me her keys and I went to the mudroom to grab my bag.

I'm strong for my size, but lifting the gear onto my back and carrying it outside took almost everything I had. With a grunt like a rabid animal (or my sister before nine in the morning), I heaved it into Mum's minivan.

I climbed into the passenger seat and buckled up just as Mum got in with a travel mug of tea for herself and a hot chocolate for me. She started the van, cranked up the heat and turned the radio to CBC news.

Boring.

"There's a bagel in the bag," she said, nodding toward her purse while the weather report told us it would be raining all week.

Rain in B.C.?

Surprise, surprise.

"I'm not hungry," I told her. I was too excited about practice to think about food.

"Well, you've got to eat something," she said, pulling onto Evergreen Drive and squinting against the headlights of another car.

"But —"

"Nugget," she said, shooting me a look that could probably wound, if not kill, "you're eating the bagel."

"J.T.," I reminded her.

"Fine. Jonathan, J.T., whoever you are today, you're eating the bagel."

It was no use arguing with a professional nutritionist. She'd probably make me wear one of her yellow food pyramid t-shirts to school if I didn't give in, so I unwrapped the bagel and took a big bite. It was excellent — lightly toasted and smeared with crunchy peanut butter. Maybe I was hungry, after all.

"Thanks, Mum."

"You're welcome," she said, with a smile. "Have you got everything you need for school?"

She was the queen of double-checking.

"Yup. My clothes are in the bag," I told her, once I'd swallowed my mouthful.

"And your Math homework?"

"It's in there," I told her, taking another bite.

"Complete?"

Uh oh.

"Completely in there," I told her, as my tongue stuck to the roof of my mouth with peanut butter.

She glanced at me. "I meant is it complete?"

"Almost."

"Almost?" she asked, slowly pulling over to the gravel shoulder, as if the rink could wait.

"What are you doing?" I gasped. It was the first day of practice! We didn't have time to waste yakking on the side of the road.

"Getting to the bottom of this." She turned to face me and I hoped her eyes wouldn't drill holes through my fore-head. "Why isn't it done?"

"It will be," I promised. "I'll finish it in Mrs. Cavanaugh's car on the way to school." After all, Kenny's mum drove so slowly, I could probably do a year's worth of homework in one trip.

"Nugget."

"J.T."

"*J.T.*," she sighed. "We've already discussed that the car is not the place for homework."

"I know, but I had to pack my bag last night and —"

"And that's not a valid excuse. Hockey is never going to come before school at our house. You know that."

I nodded.

"I can't hear you."

"I know," I told her.

"This isn't happening again. Am I right?"

"Yes."

"Good," she said, pulling back onto the road. "Listen, I know you love to play, but school is your priority." She shook her head. "Look at your Dad. Ending his hockey career took one bad judgment call and less than five seconds."

She was right, of course. Dad played right wing (just like me) for a junior team in Saskatchewan before he met her. Everyone says he would have become an NHL All-Star, for sure. But just before the scouts for none other than the *Calgary Flames* came to check him out, he got hit in the cheekbone with a puck going about a thousand kilometres an hour, and he wasn't wearing a face mask.

The puck shattered the bone and damaged his left eye so he couldn't play anymore. He was a ref for a little while after that, but his vision was messed up and it just didn't work. So that was the end of that. Of course, I knew Dad liked working at the insurance company, but not as much as he would have loved playing for the Flames.

And since his career was cut short, the McDonald family hockey legacy was resting on my shoulders. It was up to me to play hard and fast, skating circles around the competition as a right winger. It was up to me to lead the second-place Cougars to the championship.

And I wanted to!

But my puny size had always stood in the way of ending our second-place streak. My size and Coach O'Neal, that is.

Our season always came down to one big game, and I never, *ever* got to play in it.

The Shoreline Sharks were not only the top-ranked team on the island, but the biggest. And when I say big, I mean they were a bunch of bruisers who looked like professional body builders. (Okay, they might have looked more like, say, average sized fourteen-year-olds, but the rest of us were eleven.)

Because I was extra small, Coach didn't think I could handle myself on the ice against those goons. Every single year, I spent the Shoreline game watching my team lose from a front row seat on the bench.

The best seat in the house, for the worst moments of the season.

But what Coach didn't know was that while I may not have grown, after a summer of working as hard as I possibly could to prepare for the season, I was tougher and faster than I'd ever been. And I was going to play against the Sharks, no matter what.

Mum didn't seem to notice I'd stopped listening to her, and luckily, I'd heard it all before, so it wasn't hard to catch up as she was finishing. "So, if your Dad didn't have an education, he would have been out of luck. School is more important than anything else."

"I get it, Mum. But seriously, I'm never going to use *Math*."

She laughed. "Of course you are."

"Nope. I want to play for the Canucks and all hockey players have to do is skate and score."

"Is that right?" she laughed again. "How do you plan to handle your NHL salary and bonuses without Math?"

Hmm.

I hated to admit it, but she had me there.

When we got to the rink, I kissed Mum goodbye and carried my bag inside, where my buddy Kenny Cavanaugh was just ahead of me on the way to the locker room.

"Hey, Nugget," he said, glancing over his shoulder.

I took a deep breath. It was time to get the ball rolling. "J.T."

"Huh?"

"I go by J.T. now."

"Since when?"

"Since now."

Kenny paused for a second, then shrugged under the weight of his gear. "Whatever you say."

I followed him to the locker room, which smelled the way it always did: like burnt popcorn and sweat. Kind of gross, but kind of nice too.

We started pulling gear from our bags, piling helmets, gloves, pads and practice jerseys onto one of the benches. We wouldn't be allowed to use the lockers until we were in high school, and I couldn't wait.

"So?" Kenny asked, licking his palm and trying to squish one of his cowlicks. It was going to take a lot more than spit to tame that thing. It stuck up like the antenna on Mum's minivan and all it needed was a happy face bobble at the tip.

"So what?" I asked.

"So, why J.T.?"

I didn't want to tell him I thought it sounded cool and mysterious. "Those are my initials," I said.

"Gotcha," he nodded. "Jonathan."

"Yeah, Jonathan Thomas."

"J.T." He shrugged. "It works for me."

"I mean, they only call me Nugget because —"

"You're small," he finished for me.

I gritted my teeth. "Right, but it's mostly because my sister's Wendy McDonald. You know, the double fast food thing. They've been calling her *Big Mac* for as long as I can remember, but obviously instead of *Hamburger* or *Quarter Pounder*, I got stuck with . . . *Nugget*."

"Oh," Kenny said, nodding his head. "I always thought it was like a gold nugget or something, but it's actually —"

"Chicken," I told him quietly.

He shrugged. "Well, they're good with sweet and sour sauce."

Like that was going to make me feel better.

"I've spent two years being called a chicken nugget, Kenny."

He nodded, like he understood. "And you didn't like it."

I stared at him. "Would you?"

Kenny shrugged. "My brother calls me Turd, so I'm probably not the best person to ask."

I cringed. Apparently, things could have been worse.

Even so, I hoped J.T. would catch on. It suited me, and I didn't even care that my sister had already said it stood for "Just Tiny."

You know what I thought?

I thought the dumbest thing about nicknames like "Nugget" or "Minor League Midget" was that they were so obvious. I knew I was short. Everyone knew I was short. All they had to do was look at me to see the evidence stacked up and staring back at them.

"J.T.," Kenny said, interrupting my thoughts. "Earth to J.T."

"What?"

"You zoned out. I was saying I can't believe how cold it is out there." He pulled on his shin guards.

I thought so too, but told him, "This is nothing compared to where my dad grew up in Saskatchewan."

"Oh yeah?" Kenny asked, as he reached for his red and black hockey socks.

"One winter the snow got so high, Dad and my Aunt Judy could jump off the roof onto it."

"Huh," Kenny said, not as impressed as he should have been. "Well, my brother in Calgary tripped on his way to a movie last winter. Know what he tripped over?"

"What?"

"The light on the top of a taxi."

Big deal. "It fell off a cab?"

"No, dummy. The whole car was buried. The whole *road* was buried. He was walking on top of the taxi and didn't even know it."

I stopped and stared at him. "No joke?"

"No joke."

"Whew. Now that's snow."

I wished I lived somewhere back east, like Quebec, where instead of rain, it snowed like crazy and the lakes froze solid enough to skate on. No one even had to worry about paying for ice time. I wished that all I had to do was play hockey. That way, I could forget about Math, and forget school altogether.

Just play hockey.

"So, what do you think about the new guy?" Kenny asked, as he sat on the bench and started taping his stick.

I'd already taped mine the night before, since it was my favourite part of getting ready for the new season. "What new guy?" I asked, adjusting my shoulder pads.

Jeff McDaniel walked into the locker room and dumped his bag on the other bench. His sweatshirt was inside-out and there was a piece of beef jerky hanging from his mouth. Mum would have flipped if she saw that was how he started his day.

"Nice breakfast." Kenny laughed.

"What new guy?" I asked again.

"Eddie Bosko," Jeff said.

His breath smelled like the inside of Dad's slippers. After a long weekend. During a heat wave.

"Eddie Bosko?" The name sounded super familiar.

"So, now we're swimming with the Sharks, eh guys?" Colin Bechter said, joining us and dropping his overflowing bag on the floor.

"What are you talking about?" I asked.

"Did you guys hear about Eddie Bosko?" Patrick Chen asked, from the doorway.

"I know," Kenny said, rolling his eyes.

"How's it going?" David McCafferty mumbled, nodding to everyone as he came in. His hair was flat on one side, like he'd slept against the car window on the way over. He always looked half asleep.

"We're talking about Eddie Bosko," Colin told him.

"I heard," David said. "What a burn."

"What are you guys talking about?" I practically shouted, mad that I was the only one who didn't know.

"Geez! Cool your jets, Nugget," Colin said.

"J.T." Kenny told him.

"What?"

"Never mind," I growled. "Can somebody just tell me what's going on?"

"Our new player," Colin explained, "is Eddie Bosko."

"Okay," I said, still not sure what the big deal was.

Colin rolled his eyes. "Eddie Bosko from the *Shoreline Sharks*."

Oh, nuts.

That Eddie Bosko.

"What?" I croaked.

"That dude is a killer stickhandler," Jeff said, shaking his head in awe.

It couldn't be happening. It didn't make sense. "Yeah, but . . . he's a Shark," I said, quietly.

"Not anymore. His family just moved here," Kenny said. "So he'll be going to school with us too."

"The kid is massive," Jeff said, still shaking his head. "And have you felt his shoulder-checks?"

All the guys silently nodded, remembering the jolt of bodies slammed against the boards. Everybody but me, anyway. I just remembered watching him pound on us while I sat on the bench, itching to get out on the ice.

"You know, I've been thinking about it, and with him on our side now, this could end up being our best season ever," Patrick said.

"Dude," Kenny said, "he's the enemy."

Most of us nodded and got back to dressing for practice. That is, until Eddie Bosko entered the locker room. I didn't see him or hear him right away, but I felt his presence, like ice cream melting down my spine.

When I turned to face him, he looked about seven feet tall.

His hair was dark and shaggy and I swear the kid had a *mustache*. His bag, loaded with just as much stuff as mine, dangled from one of his monster paws like it weighed nothing. Like a bag of marshmallows.

I wished he didn't look so big and tough. I wished guys like Jeff and Patrick weren't happy about him joining our team.

But more than anything, I wished he wasn't a right winger too.

Chapter Two

The whole team went dead quiet when Eddie Bosko pulled a dark blue Sharks practice jersey on over his pads. I couldn't believe it. A Sharks jersey. How much nerve did the guy have?

"I'm sure Coach has a Cougars one for you," I said, both stunned and ticked off that he'd even try to wear it in our locker room.

Eddie Bosko glanced at me like I was nothing and shrugged. "I'm cool with this one."

His voice was deep, like my Dad's, and I wondered how this freak of nature could possibly be my age. All the guys looked at each other without saying anything, but I wasn't about to let him intimidate me.

"I'm actually positive he'll give you a new jersey," I said, firmly but with a smile. "I'm J.T.," I added. "Starting right winger."

"Starter, eh?" The giant smirked.

Were those *fangs*?

"Yeah," I said, sounding more sure than I felt. "So, anyway, welcome to the team."

Half the guys just stared while the other half jumped in to welcome him, like a flock of hungry seagulls going after chum. When the room quieted down again, Eddie Bosko looked each of us over carefully, without smiling.

"It wasn't a choice."

Before anyone could say a word, he lifted his skates by their laces, slipped them onto his massive shoulder and walked out of the locker room.

"What a jerk," David mumbled, yawning and rubbing his eyes.

"Huge jerk," Kenny added.

"Heavy on the huge," Colin groaned. "That guy could eat us for lunch."

"Except Nugget," David said, elbowing me. I was feeling like a real tough guy, until he added, "who'd be more of a snack."

"Very funny." I turned to zip my bag as the guys started heading for the ice.

"What are you going to do?" Kenny asked, quietly, when we were alone.

"About what?"

"Keeping your position. You know Eddie Bosko's gonna want to start."

"I know," I said, frowning.

It was my position. I was the one who'd worked for it. I was the one who'd played with these guys since I was six. Eddie Bosko couldn't just show up like some overgrown gorilla and run the whole stinkin' show!

"So?" Kenny asked.

There was only one answer, and I didn't like it one bit.

"I guess I'll be fighting for it."

* * *

Coach O'Neal handled practice like we'd never had a summer break, but I didn't mind. After all, I'd spent my vacation and early fall getting ready to play my best season ever.

When we ran drills, skating as fast as we could to the centre line and back, then to the far goal line and back, over and over again, some of the guys were gasping for breath after only three repeats.

Not me, though. I'd gone running or rollerblading almost every day for the whole two months, building up stamina. Sure, my lungs burned as I gulped freezing air and let it out in hot bursts of steam, but it felt good.

"Patrick and Kenny, you're out," Coach O'Neal shouted as I lapped them. "You too, Jeff."

The numbers dropped pretty quickly after that, as the guys who were struggling were pulled to the side. Coach sounded disappointed every time he eliminated one of his players.

"Bechter, come on!" he said, as Colin wiped out on a turn and was eliminated.

I needed to prove myself, so I kept going. I found a steady breathing pattern that matched the scrape of my blades and concentrated on keeping it up.

"Jeremy, you're done," Coach shouted, and one more dropped from the ranks.

Eventually, it was down to just me, Chris Fullerton and Eddie Bosko, who was a metre or so ahead of me. I took a deep breath and picked up my pace to catch up with him, just as Chris was called out by Coach. I stopped at the centre line, spraying flakes of ice, and raced back toward our goal.

I had to beat him.

I grunted as I reached the line and turned again.

"Go, J.T.!" Kenny shouted.

I skated as fast as I could, my legs heavy and my lungs on fire as I raced toward the far goal, Eddie Bosko right next to me. I glanced over and saw that his hair was wet with sweat just like mine, but that only made me work harder. At the line, I made my quickest turn yet, then started back.

"Last stretch!" Coach shouted down the rink.

With a burst of adrenaline, I kicked it into high gear, but so did Eddie Bosko. We were neck and neck. (Well, neck and tree stump.)

Come on, come on, come on.

I could hear the guys cheering for me, and even though most of them were shouting "Nugget," it was the thought that counted. I tried to pull ahead, desperate to win, but the giant was right next to me. Panting, I gave it everything I had, but at the very last second Eddie Bosko shot ahead and crossed the goal line a couple of feet ahead of me.

Nuts.

I slammed into the boards so hard the Plexiglas wobbled.

"Nice hustle, guys," Coach said, his clipboard tucked under his arm so he could clap for us.

Not nice enough, though. I looked at Eddie Bosko, glad to see he was trying to catch his breath, too.

"Man, you hauled," Kenny whispered.

"He beat me," I whispered between gasps.

"You were close."

I didn't say anything.

Close only counts in horseshoes and hand grenades, my grandpa always told me.

"So," Coach O'Neal said. "It looks like we've got our work cut out for us."

My knees were shaking and I could taste salty sweat on my upper lip.

"Our first game is a little over a week away, guys, so I'm expecting you to step up." He looked at my panting enemy. "As I'm sure you've noticed, we have a new player this year. If you haven't met him yet, this is Eddie Bosko."

We were silent and I knew the guys were thinking about what Eddie had said about not choosing to join the team.

Coach continued, "He used to be a Shark, but now he's a Cougar. So let's make him welcome."

Patrick and Jeff smiled at Eddie, but the monster's face was as blank as the pages of my Math homework.

"Eddie," Coach added, "I've got a practice jersey for you in my office. Come and see me before you leave today."

Ha!

"Told you so," I muttered, loud enough for only Kenny to hear.

He smiled.

Coach put out a bunch of cones and for the next twenty minutes we started at one end of the rink, swerving in and out of them with a puck. Each time we made it through, we took a shot on the empty net.

I didn't miss once, but neither did Eddie Bosko.

He beat me in three other drills and even though I was working as hard as I could, I only beat him in one. By the time we were down to the last ten minutes of practice, I'd had way too much of the new guy.

"Do we have time for a scrimmage, Coach?" Jeff asked, glancing at the clock above us. It had been smashed by flying pucks so many times it had a metal cage over it.

"We always have time for a scrimmage," Coach said, laughing.

He divided us into teams and tossed the red pinnies to my group. We only had a few seconds to scramble into position.

I wasn't fast enough and ended up at left wing, eye to eye with Eddie Bosko at the centre line. (Well, eye to chest, anyway.) My heart pounded as the puck dropped and Kenny, who was on the other team, took possession. I turned and skated toward our goal, ready to defend it while Kenny passed to Jeff, who got a breakaway. Once Jeff got close, he fired off a shot that missed the crease completely.

"What was that?" Eddie Bosko grunted from behind me.

My lucky break.

I raced around the back of the net, scooping the puck with my stick and taking off toward the far goal. Nothing on earth felt better than racing past the centre line, knowing there was a chance of scoring. It didn't matter that it wasn't a real game, or that there was no one in the stands, because all I cared about was playing.

My blades sliced the ice and my stick worked the puck toward Jeremy. He was stuck in goal (which I knew he hated) and doing his best to figure out what kind of a crazy move I was about to pull. I faked left, then right, glancing every couple of seconds at the top right corner of the goal.

My target.

I'd practised the shot with a tennis ball all summer long, and I'd been itching to make it on the ice.

This is gonna be sweet.

I pushed the puck a little to the left and prepared to take the shot, which was lined up perfectly. Forget the drills and forget Eddie Bosko. My season would be off to an awesome start.

At least it *could* have been, if a stick hadn't come out of nowhere, cutting in front of me.

Eddie Bosko first whipped the puck out of my control, then out of reach completely.

"Don't mind me," he said, swooping past with a smirk.

By the time I closed my gaping mouth, he was gone. By the time I turned around, he was halfway to our net. By the time I took off after him, he had already *scored*. And that's when I knew that no matter how hard I had worked and how badly I wanted it, defending my spot as a starter wasn't going to be easy.

* * *

My day didn't improve when I got to school and realized the Math problems I'd hurried through in the backseat of Mrs. Cavanaugh's car weren't even part of our homework assignment.

"Mr. McDonald," Mr. Holloway said, shaking his head when he saw my mistake, "even the great Mr. Gretzky once had to pay attention in Math class."

"Only once?" I tried to joke, which turned out to be a bad idea.

"I'm not amused, Mr. McDonald, and I doubt your mother will see the humour at parent-teacher interviews next week."

"Can I make it up?" I asked.

He looked at me over the top of his glasses. It was a long, cold stare that made me wish I hadn't asked. "You can try. I'll give you an extra assignment at the end of class."

I slouched in my seat. Great. I'd actually asked for more homework, and gotten it.

Someone knocked on the door and Mr. Holloway left for

a minute before returning with none other than Mr. Right Wing.

Couldn't I have one measly second away from the guy?

"Class, we have a new student with us today. Eddie Bosko has just moved to Cutter Bay from Shoreline."

Eddie scanned the room and even though he must have recognized me, he barely made eye contact before moving on to the next kid.

Jerk.

"Mr. Bosko, I see we have a vacant seat at the back, next to our friend Mr. McDonald."

I thought he had to be kidding, but he wasn't, and even added, "Please try not to let his study habits rub off on you."

Oh, brother.

The giant walked down the aisle toward me, smirking again. I cleared my throat as he sat down and dumped his knapsack on the floor. Deciding my best bet was to just be friendly, I whispered, "Hey."

He glanced at me but didn't say anything. Instead he unzipped his bag and pulled out a black binder.

Big jerk.

I flipped to a fresh page in my notebook and tried to listen to what Mr. Holloway was saying about working out percentages but, as usual, I couldn't get into it. No matter what Mum said, I knew Math didn't matter. And even if way off in the future I did need to figure something out, that's what calculators were for.

I looked out the window and wished that I was outside, instead of stuck at a stupid desk. I wished I was at the rink or at Pro-Sports, checking out their new gear.

When Dad and I bought my new skates there, I'd seen

a killer helmet. It was red and black, just like my Cougar uniform, with flaming lightning bolts all over it. It was *so* cool, but *so* expensive. In fact, the price was almost three times what mine cost.

"Mr. McDonald?" Mr. Holloway asked.

When I looked toward the front of the room, I saw that the whole class was turned around, staring at me.

Oops.

"Yes?" I hoped he hadn't already asked me a question about the problem on the board.

"I hope I'm not interrupting your reverie."

My what?

"Perhaps you'd like to share your thoughts with the class?"

"Uh . . ."

"Perhaps we can incorporate your *daydream* into today's lesson."

A couple of kids snickered and Eddie Bosko smirked again. I was beginning to think that was the only thing he could do.

Well, that and play hockey. Practice was bad enough, so I was in no mood to be humiliated in front of him in Math class, too. I thought about what Mr. Holloway had said for a couple of seconds.

Aha!

"Actually," I said, "we probably could."

My teacher's eyes bugged out. "Is that right?"

"Yeah."

"Pardon me?" he asked, frowning.

"Sorry, I meant yes."

"Thank you. Please proceed."

"Well, there's this helmet at Pro-Sports I want, a hockey

helmet. It costs a hundred and eighty-nine dollars —"

"Quite the helmet," Mr. Holloway said, eyebrows raised.

"It is," I assured him. "It has this awesome flaming pattern in red and —"

"Save it for art class, Mr. McDonald. Let's discuss the numbers."

"Okay, so my weekly allowance is ten dollars, and I'm trying to figure out —"

"How long it will take you to save the money?"

I nodded. "The tricky part, is we bought my skates there last month, so we have a coupon for five percent off our next purchase."

"Wonderful," Mr. Holloway said, moving toward the board. "Let's work through this, class."

And that's exactly what we did. The nerds at the front did most of the number crunching, but I followed along better than I usually did, since I actually cared about the answer, for once.

When the results were in, I found out that I'd be able to get my beloved helmet . . . when hockey season was over.

Instead of smirking, this time Eddie Bosko snorted.

Just perfect.

Chapter Three

When the school day finally ended, I walked home with Kenny. He only lived a couple of blocks away from me, so we usually went together. The wind was whipping leaves all over the place and for once I was glad it wasn't Saturday. Dad and I usually raked the yard on the weekends.

"I almost forgot," Kenny said, "Mum wanted me to ask if I can get a ride to practice tomorrow." He pulled a Red Wings tuque out of his pack. It would probably stop the wind, but nothing could control that crazy cowlick.

"I'll have to ask, but I'm pretty sure you can."

Mum only liked driving carpool for kids who were guaranteed to be on time, and Kenny could be . . . iffy. It had something to do with his snooze button.

"So, what did you think about practice?" he asked, slipping the bright red tuque on and centering the team logo by feel.

The answer was easy. "It stunk."

Kenny's hands dropped to his sides and he groaned, "I know. Man, why did Eddie Bosko have to come here?"

"Yeah. Why couldn't he have gone to Nanaimo, or Courtney —"

"Or Vancouver," Kenny added.

"Or Tokyo."

"Yeah," he said, laughing. "Tokyo would work."

I didn't say anything more. I was too busy thinking about how much everything had changed in one measly day. Kenny kicked a rock every couple of steps, and I shoved my hands deep in my pockets, wondering how I was going to compete against a beast like Eddie Bosko.

"You watching the game tomorrow night?" Kenny asked.

I turned to stare at him. "Duh. Canucks against your stinkin' Red Wings? Like I'd miss it."

He punched me in the arm for the insult, but smiled. "That's what I figured. My dad just bought a new flat screen if you want to come over."

"That would be awesome . . . but I can't hang out on a school night." Sometimes it seemed like my whole life was rules, rules and more rules.

"Gotcha," Kenny nodded. "Hey, did you hear about that contest on PUCK Radio?"

I shook my head. "My parents only listen to the news and classical music."

"Ugh. Well, see if you can check it out tonight. There's a show on from eight to nine and they're doing a trivia contest for two weeks."

"Hockey trivia?"

"It's PUCK Radio, Nugget."

"J.T.," I reminded him. "What do you win?"

"Cool stuff, like a signed NHL jersey —"

"Signed by who?" I asked. Man, if it was Jean Ducette, I

would have a heart attack, right there on the sidewalk.

"Sean Carter."

"Hmph," I snorted. "Nobody likes the Penguins."

"I do," Kenny said, elbowing me.

"Okay, *one person* likes the Penguins."

Kenny shrugged. "There's other prizes too, like sticks, helmets —"

"Seriously?" I asked, smiling at the thought. A helmet would be pretty awesome. What if it was the flaming one I'd been dreaming about? What if I didn't have to find ways to work around the house to save up for it? What if I just won it?

"Anyway, it's been building up over the past few days, with bigger prizes every day. Someone will win the grand prize on Sunday."

Grand prize? There was something better than signed jerseys and helmets? "What is it?"

Kenny cleared his throat, then leaned over and started slapping his knees really fast. I waved as the O'Donnells drove by, Kate and Nick's noses pressed against the windows as they stared at us. I smiled like Kenny wasn't totally nuts, which wasn't easy.

"What are you doing?" I finally asked.

"A drum roll," he said, slapping even faster.

"Knock it off," I told him, laughing. "What do you win?"

He stood straight and grinned at me. "Tickets to a Canucks game."

"No way!" I almost screamed.

"Against the Flames."

"No way!" I shouted, even louder. I was so excited, my hands were sweating.

"Good seats, too."

"That's awesome," I said, shaking my head.

I'd never seen an NHL game. Sure, I'd watched on TV, but that wasn't the same. I'd even been to Vancouver a few times, and we drove by Rogers Arena when the Canucks were playing, but I'd never, ever, been to a real live game. I tried to imagine walking into the stadium, surrounded by the rest of the fans. We'd all be wearing blue and green, shouting at the top of our lungs.

"That's not even the best part," Kenny said.

I stopped walking, thinking I'd heard him wrong. How could anything be better than a real live Canucks game? Against the Flames, no less. "What are you talking about?"

"Well, you get two tickets to the game and . . ." he wiggled his eyebrows.

"What?"

"It's big," he teased.

"What is it?"

"Huge."

"Kenny," I warned.

"Guess."

I had no idea. Could it be a chance to meet one of the players? What if it was Jean Ducette? What if I got to shake hands with my hero? I'd pass out, for sure.

"I'm waiting," Kenny sang.

"Just tell me."

He folded his arms across his chest and made me wait a few more seconds. I was ready to tackle him and I think he could see it in my eyes, because that's when he blew me away with five magical words.

"A shot from centre ice."

What? My head buzzed. "Are you *kidding* me?"

"Nope. And if you score, you get money and a bunch of autographed Canucks stuff."

"Seriously?"

"Seriously," he nodded. "PUCK Radio at eight o'clock."

I was so excited I could barely breathe, and the second Kenny turned off on Arbutus Street I hightailed it home. When I got there I ran up the back steps and threw open the kitchen door.

"Geez!" my sister Wendy snapped. She was on the phone as usual. "Close the door! It's freezing out there, Nugget."

I didn't bother reminding her about J.T. I had bigger things to think about. I tossed my knapsack into the mudroom, poured myself an ice-cold glass of milk and went straight upstairs.

My door was covered with the WARNING: CONTAMINATED AREA, DANGER and DO NOT ENTER signs I'd pulled out of my Christmas stocking the year before. I had to shove hard to open it because of the pile of sweats and jeans I kept dropping on the floor instead of into the laundry basket.

My walls were plastered with posters of Jean Ducette, and other great players too, like Roberto Luongo and Henrik Sedin. My bulletin board was covered with cutouts from the sports pages, a few team stickers and the Canucks schedule for the season. Right next to the bulletin board was my bookcase. On the bottom shelf were the things I needed for school, like a dictionary, spare pencils and junk like that. On the second shelf were a couple of puny hockey trophies from when I was little, along with my Atom team photo.

But what I really needed was on the top shelf, mixed in with the rest of my growing hockey library. I had biographies of some of the old players, like Gordie Howe, Maurice "The Rocket" Richard and Bobby Orr, as well as histories of almost half the teams in the league.

But I also had the key to winning the contest and I smiled when I pulled my hockey encyclopedia off the shelf.

Shoot! Third Edition.

They'd come out with a fourth edition almost a month earlier, and I couldn't wait to get it, but it was on backorder at Chapters.

I straightened my blankets and flopped onto my bed, ready to start studying. Sure, I already knew a ton of trivia and facts, but I also knew that with the prizes PUCK Radio was giving out, the questions wouldn't be easy. I'd have to tune in every night, no matter what, because practise made perfect. That was something I knew from working on my slapshot all summer.

I'd have to read *Shoot! Third Edition* from cover to cover, at least twice.

Just as I settled in to get started, Mum knocked on the door. "Jonathan?"

"Come in," I called to her.

It took her a couple of tries to push the door open, and when she made it into the room, she immediately put her hands on her hips. "Kind of a fire hazard, hon."

"I'll clean it up," I told her, for probably the seventh time in the past two weeks.

"I know you will. Today."

"Okay," I sighed. I'd have to fit it in around my hockey studying, somehow.

"I didn't know you were home. Wendy said you bar-relled through the kitchen."

"I was in a hurry."

"Apparently," she said, raising an eyebrow. "You didn't even stop by the den to say hello."

"Sorry," I told her, hoping we could wrap up the conversation quickly so I could get back to work.

"How was school?" she asked, crossing her arms and leaning against the doorway like she might stay there . . . forever.

"Okay."

"And practice?"

"Fine."

"One word answers aren't going to do the trick."

What *would* do the trick? "School was fine."

"What are you doing?" Mum asked.

It was kind of a weird question, considering I was lying on my bed, glued to an open book. "Reading," I said, then remembered she'd want more words. "It's a hockey book."

"I can see that." She frowned. "I thought your English class was reading *Over the Moon*?"

They probably were. "Uh, yeah. I'm a couple of chapters into it." Well, more like a couple of pages, but close enough.

"Don't you think *Over the Moon* is what you should be reading now?" I knew from experience that it might have sounded like a question, but it really wasn't.

"I guess so," I sighed.

She stepped into the hallway for a second, then came back with my knapsack. "I brought your books up so you wouldn't need binoculars to do your homework."

"Thanks," I said, reaching for the bag. How was I supposed to win a shot from centre ice if I had to spend all my time on assigned reading?

* * *

By dinnertime, I'd only read three pages of the stupid book because I'd been too busy sneaking peeks at *Shoot! Third Edition* and daydreaming about scoring from centre ice.

When Mum called me to the table for the second time, it was a lot louder than the first, so I rolled off my bed and went downstairs.

"Salmon," Wendy said, as I sat down next to her.

It was one of my favourites, especially when Mum made wild rice to go with it, which she had. While the four of us ate, we talked about what had happened that day, like we always did.

When I went to Kenny or Colin's houses for dinner, the kids ate in front of the TV in the living room and the parents ate at the kitchen table, which was too weird.

I liked dinner our way, even if Wendy never stopped talking.

"Can you please pass the rice?" I asked Dad.

He handed me the bowl and I loaded up my plate, then grabbed a roll and sliced off a bit of butter.

"I don't see any salad on your plate, Jonathan," Mum said, while my sister was in mid-sentence.

Wendy handed me the bowl with a dirty look. "Mum, I'm kind of in the middle of something, here," she whined.

I scooped salad onto my plate and added some of Mum's homemade Italian dressing.

"Go ahead, Wend," Dad said, reaching over to pat her arm.

"Okay, so Danielle says she won't go to the dance unless Chris asks her, but he already asked Lisa and —"

"Which one is Lisa again?" Mum asked.

"Blond hair, plays ringette."

"Right, okay," Mum nodded as she chewed.

"So anyway, Lisa wants to go with Jason, who is kind of seeing Carmen and —"

"This is like a soap opera," Dad whispered to me.

"A bad one," I told him.

"Do you mind?" Wendy asked, staring at me. "I always listen to your hockey stories, so I'd appreciate it if you'd do the same for me."

"This is about to turn into a hockey story?" I asked, knowing that wasn't what she meant.

"Geez, Nugget, can I just —"

"J.T.," I reminded her.

Wendy rolled her eyes. "You know what? You don't get to pick your own nickname."

"Why not?" I asked, taking a bite of my salmon, which was awesome.

"Because that's not how it works."

Dad turned to look at me. "You want us to call you J.T.?"

"Where have you *been*, Dad?" Wendy asked.

He didn't answer her, but asked me, "You don't like Nugget?"

Was he kidding? Who on earth would want to be called Nugget? "No way," I said, through a mouthful of food.

"Gross," Wendy groaned. "I don't need to see that."

"Then don't look," I told her. I was ready for a change of subject. "Hey, there's a new contest on PUCK —"

"Can I finish my story?" Wendy snapped.

I doubted it actually had an ending, since they never seemed to.

"Go ahead, honey," Mum said, but I could tell she was about as interested as I was in whether Katie-Ali-Jenny-Susie-Lisa-Sarah went to the dance with Jason-David-Chad-Peter-Gavin.

Wendy chattered away for the next few minutes, while I tested myself by trying to remember the starting lineups for every team in the Northwestern Division. It was harder than I expected.

I cleared the table, since Wendy had set it, and when I carried the plates into the kitchen, I saw that Mum had made dessert.

We never had dessert on weeknights!

Even better? It was apple crisp.

I ate mine slowly, enjoying every single bite, and watched the clock as it inched closer to eight o'clock, glad that my rotten day was almost behind me.

As I chewed, Mum started telling us about her day.

"There's a new woman at work, who just moved here from either Comox or Shoreline, I can't remember which. Anyway, she has two boys, around your ages."

"I saw him in homeroom," Wendy said. "Shane something." She shrugged. "He's not as cute as Tyler Bradshaw."

"But who is?" Dad said, laughing.

"Very funny," Wendy said.

I was stuck on the name of the Oilers' goalie, amazed I'd forgotten. I chewed slowly as I went through the alphabet, trying to come up with it.

"Anyway," Mum said, "the older one plays rugby and the younger one recently won a provincial Math award."

The goalie's last name was McNeal or something. Maybe McDougall? McAllister?

"A Math award?" Dad asked, glancing over at me. "Impressive."

"Yes, and apparently this boy has done some tutoring in the past, so I told his mother we'd be interested. Isn't that right Jonathan?"

I almost had it. I could practically see the guy's face.

"Sean McCallum!" I finally announced, totally relieved.

"What's wrong with you?" Wendy asked.

"Jonathan?" Mum asked, looking worried.

"Sorry," I said, shaking my head to warm my brain up a bit. "What did you say?"

"*Math*, honey. We know you've been struggling and this seems like the perfect solution, dropped right into our laps!"

Perfect solution?

"Solution for what?" I asked.

"This boy," Mum told me. "This Eddie Bosko. He's going to be your Math tutor."

Chapter Four

I dropped my fork with a clatter, spraying bits of apple crisp onto Wendy's shirt.

"Nice one, Nugget," she snarled, racing into the kitchen to clean herself off.

Oh, brother. It was apples and oats, not toxic waste.

"What's wrong?" Mum asked.

What's wrong? My arch-enemy was going to "help" me!

"I don't need a tutor," I muttered. "And besides, shouldn't a tutor be like . . . a teenager?"

"He's a prodigy," Mum said.

"Okay, I don't even know what that is."

"A young genius," Dad said.

I rolled my eyes. "Great. Next I'm going to find out he's Jean Ducette's nephew."

"What?" Mum asked.

"Nothing," I sighed.

"Gord?" Mum looked to Dad for backup.

He swallowed his last bite of crisp. "There's nothing wrong with getting some help, kiddo."

"But —"

"Math is tough, and it's going to get tougher in the next couple of years. I think a tutor is a good way to prepare for that."

"But Eddie Bosko?" I groaned, then realized that saying the name out loud only made it worse.

"You've met him?" Mum asked, smiling like I'd just told her I aced a Math test.

"Yeah," I sighed. "He's on the team."

"Well," she said, smiling even wider. "That's why I thought it was a good idea."

"That's exactly why it's *not* a good idea," I told her.

"What do you mean?" Mum asked, frowning.

"He's . . ." I wasn't sure how to explain it nicely, so I just went from the gut. "He's a knuckle-dragging gorilla who probably eats second graders *and* their Math homework for breakfast."

I heard Dad cough, but when I turned to look, I saw that he was actually choking on a laugh.

It wasn't funny.

"I'm serious," I told them. "He's a total thug."

"He's an eleven-year-old, Jonathan," Mum said, shaking her head.

"Trapped in a twenty-five-year-old's body."

"It can't be that bad," Dad said, still chuckling.

"Oh, it is. It definitely is. He's a huge jerk. He thinks he's going to take over as starting right wing and he actually showed up to practice in a Sharks jersey today, if you can believe it. He's just a big, stinking jerk."

"Who is?" Wendy asked, joining us at the table with big wet marks all over her shirt.

"Eddie Bosko," I grunted.

"Right, Bosko," Wendy repeated, scrunching her face up to think about it for a second. "Shane Bosko. Dark hair, dark eyes —"

"Does he look like the Missing Link?" I asked. "Because his brother does."

"That's enough," Mum said, and her tone was almost as dangerous as the look she was giving me. "You are struggling in Math and need some help. This Eddie Bosko is a prodigy —"

"Do you have to keep bringing that up?" I muttered.

"And he's a new kid in a brand new town. He's probably lonely and —"

I couldn't help snorting. The gorilla? Lonely?

Mom frowned at me. "You can both help each other out, Jonathan."

"Give it a chance," Dad said, smiling. "And don't worry about having another right winger on the team. You're a great player and a little competition might even boost your game a bit." He smiled. "Nothing wrong with that."

"Maybe," I said, still doubtful.

"So, it's settled," Mum said, stacking her empty dessert bowl on top of mine so I could load them both in the dishwasher. "And now it's time for you to tackle your homework."

But when I walked into the kitchen and glanced at the calendar hanging on the wall, I saw that it was time to tackle something else.

It was the first of the month and there was still a chance my rotten day could improve.

Wendy came in to use the phone while I hurried to finish loading the dishwasher. When I was done I dug around the pens, tape and junk in the drawer under the microwave before I found my ruler. Once I had it in my hand, I was ready for action.

"Yes!" I said, waving the little wooden stick.

Wendy stared at me like I was some kind of an alien, then shook her head. "It's nothing," she said into the phone. "Just my brother, being eleven."

I ignored her and raced to the open doorway. "Hey Mum!" I shouted.

"Can you keep it down?" Wendy called after me. "You're such a *dork*, Nugget."

"J.T.," I turned to correct her.

"Whatever," she sighed, rolling her eyes.

"Mum!" I shouted again.

"Where's the fire?" Mum asked, from the upstairs hallway. She was holding a half-folded towel and probably had three hundred more waiting for her in the laundry room. Wendy took more showers than my whole hockey team put together.

"It's the first," I said, flashing the ruler and a grin.

Mum's lips tightened for a second, then she gave me a smile that seemed a bit stiff. "Hey, why don't we do it next month. That way you'll have a whole sixty days to measure, all at once."

"Mum," I sighed.

"Okay, okay," she said, giving the towel one more fold and putting it on the top shelf in the linen closet.

"Yes!" I couldn't wait.

Mum followed me into the kitchen, where I stood in my usual spot, next to the fridge. I made sure my heels and shoulder blades were as close to the wall as I could get.

"Stand still, Nugget," she whispered, placing the ruler on top of my head and reaching for a pencil.

"J.T.," I reminded her again. The nickname sure wasn't catching on like I'd hoped.

I crossed my fingers for three centimetres, or maybe even four.

"Right," she said, squinting as she made a mark.

So far, drinking milk wasn't helping and neither were stretching exercises or "thinking tall," and that stunk.

"You're wiggling," Mum said.

"Sorry," I whispered, then held my breath.

If you flipped through our photo album, the first thing you'd notice was that in every single team picture since I started playing, I was sitting on the ice in front of everybody else. While they stood in a row behind me, I was cross-legged, holding the Cutter Bay Cougars sign in my lap. That's because if the photographer lined me up next to the rest of the guys, I would have looked like the team mascot.

I'd been waiting for the growth spurt Mum kept promising for about three years, but nothing was happening. And I mean *nothing*. After all, we kept track.

I crossed my fingers even tighter as Mum stepped closer to the fresh pencil mark to write the date. I didn't turn around to look, figuring it was probably bad luck.

"So?" I finally asked.

"Mmmm . . . a pinch," she said, frowning a little.

That wasn't good. "A pinch or a smidge?" I asked her.

She hesitated. "Well, it might be closer to a smidge, hon."

I whipped around to check my latest measurement.

Nuts!

There was barely any space for Mum to write, because the new line and date was in the exact same spot as the month before. I was the same stinking height as thirty days ago! That wasn't a smidge!

Of course, it could have been worse. Sometimes she had to measure me twice because it actually looked like I'd shrunk, and that was enough to keep me up at night. In seven months, I'd only grown two centimetres, and no matter how nicely Mum told me what a big change that was, two measly centimetres was nowhere near enough to make a difference.

"Great," I groaned.

Ella Patterson and I were tied as the shortest kids in my grade. And even though we were the exact same height, she had the advantage. When she wore certain shoes or piled her hair on top of her head in a crazy bun thing, she was definitely taller.

What was I supposed to do, wear super-thick socks? Spike my hair?

"I'm sorry, honey," Mum said, rubbing my back. After a minute she added, "I really think we should start doing this every two or three months."

"No way," I said stubbornly.

"Jonathan, it's not worth getting upset over."

I looked at her like she was crazy and she pulled me into a tight hug. I let her do it because sometimes you have to let Mums give you a squeeze. (And because I liked it.)

"You're way taller than you were last year," she whispered.

"So's the front lawn," I muttered.

Sometimes I hoped the growing I'd been missing out on would catch up with me all at once. I dreamed I'd wake up one morning and when I rolled out of bed, the floor would look like it was an escalator ride away. Even better, I'd be able to reach the kitchen cupboards without that stupid wooden stool.

Sure, I knew that if I grew a bunch overnight I'd be awkward and uncoordinated, with zero control over my limbs. But if that magical miracle happened, believe me, I would figure out a way to adapt. If I had my turbo growth spurt, I'd tower over the kids at the bus stop and Mr. Su, who taught grade six P.E. and coached boys' basketball, would be following me down the hallway during lunch hour, begging me to try out. Or maybe he'd skip the tryouts and automatically put me in as a starter because he was so awestruck by my mutant, *Guinness Book of World Records* height.

Of course, it goes without saying that I didn't want to grow so I could play basketball.

After all, hockey was my life.

I could forget everything else when I was on the ice. Just like that morning, when I was out of breath, sweaty and feeling awesome. When I played, I was totally happy. It didn't matter if we were running drills or beating the Lewis Lions (we always won by a landslide), or if there were only a couple of mums in the stands, sipping coffee and talking to each other instead of watching us practise. I could pretend I was at Rogers Arena, wearing a Canucks jersey and skating my tail off to win the Stanley Cup.

"Let me guess," Dad said, opening the fridge. "Six centimetres?"

"I wish," I groaned.

"Don't worry," he said, pulling out a carton of milk. He put it on the counter before patting my head. "You're getting there, Nugget."

"J.T.," I reminded him as he filled a glass.

"J.T.," he repeated, with a wink.

Wendy finally hung up the phone, checked the wall, then turned to face me. "You need to get over it, *J.T.* Enough about your stupid height."

Easy for her to say. My sister was already taller than Mum and worried about hitting six feet by seventeen. She was the star of the high school volleyball team.

"I know, but —"

"It's about speed and skill," she said.

"I have speed and skill," I told her.

"So what are you complaining about?"

"Wendy," Mum interrupted, with a warning tone. "Can you please finish folding the laundry upstairs for me?"

My sister started toward the door while I stared at the wall and wished the pencil mark was about a foot higher.

"If size means that much, maybe you should forget hockey and be a jockey," she said as she walked by.

"Maybe you should be a giraffe," I muttered.

She stopped in her tracks and glared at me. "What did you say?"

"Nothing," I told her, knowing from years of experience how easily she could pin me.

* * *

Back in my room, I tried to shake off my frustration and disappointment. Maybe I'd grow a bit extra in the next month to make up for it. Anything could happen, right? My day had been proof of that, considering King Kong was about to become my Math tutor.

I flopped on my bed and made it through the first two chapters of *Over the Moon*, totally surprised when I kind of liked it. In fact, I actually cared what would happen next and probably would have read even more, but I knew there was Math homework to be done.

Our assignment was a whole page of percentage calculations, and of course I had the make-up homework to deal with too. I spent almost an hour messing around with the stupid percentages, and my brain felt like it might explode. When I finished, I wasn't sure about all of my answers, but figured if I got half right, that would be good enough.

Fifty percent was a passing grade, after all.

I was just about to get started on my make-up assignment when I saw that it was three minutes past eight.

Nuts!

I pushed my chair back from my desk, grabbed *Shoot! Third Edition*, and ran down to the kitchen.

Wendy was leaning against the wall, yakking on the phone again. I dragged the stool across the room and climbed onto it so I could reach the radio on top of the fridge.

"What are you doing?" Wendy snapped.

It seemed obvious. "Turning on the radio."

"I'm on the *phone*, Nugget."

"It's *cordless*, Wendy."

"Nothing," she muttered into the phone as she left the room. "Just my annoying little brother."

I turned the dial until I found PUCK Radio and sat down at the table with my book and a notepad, ready to roll. After a commercial for Mattress Land, some guy named Big Danny Donlin came on the air, talking about the Anaheim Ducks trading Yuri Karanov for Paul McFarland *and* Chris Marchand.

It took a few minutes for him to mention the trivia contest, and when he did, I scrawled the number to call on my notepad.

The phone! Wendy was hogging the stupid phone!

Why couldn't my family join the rest of the planet and get cell phones? I knew the answer, of course. I could practically hear Mum's voice in my head: "Because texting rots the brain."

I looked around the kitchen in a panic until I heard Big Danny Donlin's voice again. "Remember, folks, you can only win once."

I stopped in my tracks, realizing I didn't need the phone to call in for some random hockey book or jersey. Not when I could wait for a chance at the game tickets and a shot from centre ice.

I let out the breath I'd been holding.

Whew.

In the meantime, I figured the questions leading up to the big one would be the perfect practice for me.

After another batch of commercials, Big Danny Donlin was back. "Okay, sports fans, it's time for tonight's trivia question. Are you ready?"

"Yes," I said to the empty room.

"What are you doing?" Dad asked, from behind me.

"Shh. It's a contest," I whispered, pointing to the radio.

"Okay," Dad whispered back as he passed me to pour himself a glass of water.

"Tonight's question," Big Danny Donlin said, "is for a Canucks sweatshirt." The sound of a cheering crowd came through the speakers. "We're looking for caller number seven to tell us what team Bobby Hull played for before he joined the Winnipeg Jets."

I whipped open *Shoot! Third Edition* and started flipping through pages.

Nuts!

I was on a waiting list for the Bobby Hull biography at the public library.

"The Chicago Blackhawks," Dad said, leaning against the counter with his water.

I looked up from the book to stare at him. "Are you sure?"

"Yes," he said, laughing. "I've been a hockey fan for a long time, son. I'm sure."

We sat in silence, waiting for the seventh caller to get through.

"PUCK Radio, this is Big Danny Donlin."

"Hi Danny, this is Mike from Saanich."

"Mike from Saanich, have you got an answer to win this Canucks sweatshirt?"

"Was it the Rangers?"

A buzzer blasted through the speakers.

"Ouch! Sorry, Mike. Next caller."

"The Chicago Blackhawks," Dad said again, shaking his head.

"This is Jim from Nanaimo."

"Hey Jim," Big Danny Donlin said. "For a brand new Canucks sweatshirt, what's your answer?"

"The Chicago Blackhawks."

Bells and whistles filled the room. "Ladies and gentlemen, we have a winner!"

"You were right," I said, smiling at Dad.

"I'm not just a pretty face," Dad said, with a shrug.

"The contest is on every night."

"Interesting," Dad said, grinning as he started to leave. Just before the doorway, he bowed and said in a deep voice, "Thank you, ladies and gentlemen. I'll be here all week."

Oh, brother.

I got myself a glass of milk and went upstairs to work on the extra Math assignment, but it wasn't long before I was reading *Shoot! Third Edition* instead. Where was that stinking fourth edition? I *needed* it.

For every thing I knew about hockey, there were probably a hundred I didn't. The very first trivia question had already shown me that. Sure, I knew lots of stats for my favourite players, and I knew more than any of my friends about the old guys from the books I'd read. But if the sweat-shirt question was that tough, would I really know the answer for the grand prize?

I skipped brushing my teeth, put on my pyjamas and climbed into bed. I slowly turned the pages, reading about the old days, when the Canadiens were first nicknamed the Habs and Anaheim didn't even have a team. Then I read up on specific players, like Mario Lemieux, Sergei Federov, and, of course, Wayne Gretzky, which got me daydreaming.

What if I wasn't only an NHL player, but a legend? What would it feel like to have my picture on the cover of a magazine? To see my last name on a fan's jersey? To be asked for an autograph? What if my family was in the stands, jumping up and down, cheering me on as I fought for the Stanley Cup? Man, I'd be excited enough to just watch a game, but to be a player?

That would be the most awesome thing on the planet.

As my eyelids started to get droopy and the words were blurring together, there was a light knock on my door.

"Are you still awake?" Mum asked, opening it. "It's after ten, honey."

"I was just reading," I mumbled as my eyes closed.

"You've got practice in the morning, Jonathan. You need to get some sleep."

"I will."

"Is your homework all done?"

"Mmmhmm." I hadn't finished the extra Math assign-ment, but I could probably do it at recess or something.

"Have you packed your bag for practice?"

I hadn't, but I could easily grab my gear in the morning. "Mmmhmm."

I felt her hand stroke my forehead then push my hair to the side so she could give me a kiss. "Goodnight, my little nugget," she whispered.

For once, I didn't mind the nickname.

Nugget McDonald shoots and . . . he scores!

I pulled the blankets up to my neck and turned out my reading light, the stats for teams and players still spinning through my head.

It had been a long, brutal day and I could have easily slept for a hundred years, but my alarm was set for five a.m.

Chapter Five

When my alarm went off, my eyelids seemed to be stuck together, like someone had attacked me in the middle of the night with a glue stick. I rubbed them hard and rolled out of bed.

"Are you up?" Mum asked, rapping her knuckles on my door.

"Mrmph," was all I could say.

"Let's get moving, Jonathan," she called from farther down the hallway.

Usually I had no problem getting up for practice, but that morning, it was tough. I felt like all the stuff that was bugging me, from Eddie Bosko to Math trouble, was wrapped around my ankles, and it was hard to lift my feet.

The bathroom light was way too bright and I had to squint to brush my teeth but luckily, the shower was the perfect temperature. That is, until someone flushed the downstairs toilet.

"Blargh!" I choked, plastering myself against the tile while I reached to turn the burning hot water off.

Clean enough, I thought, even though I didn't have all the shampoo out of my hair. I'd been awake for less than ten minutes, and I already knew it wasn't going to be my day.

When I made it back to my room, I threw on my clothes, then hurried down to the mudroom to pack my hockey gear. I crammed it into my bag as fast as I could, so Mum wouldn't know I hadn't taken care of it the night before. I found everything I needed but my red and black striped hockey socks. I ran back up to my room and didn't see them anywhere. I should have just packed the night before!

"Are you ready?" Mum called up the stairs.

"Almost!"

"I'm trying to sleep!" Wendy shouted from behind her closed door.

"Sorry," I called back.

"Don't be *sorry*, be *quiet*."

"Take it easy, Wend," Dad said through her door as he passed it. "Nugget, Mum's waiting."

"I know. I'm coming."

Where were the stupid socks? I checked under the bed, in my school bag and even in the legs of the jeans I'd dumped on the floor, but I couldn't find them anywhere.

"It's five-thirty!" Mum called from the kitchen.

"And I'm still trying to sleep!" Wendy shouted.

"I'm coming," I muttered, giving up the search and heading back downstairs.

When I got to the kitchen, my packed lunch was on the table, waiting for me. Next to it was a peanut butter sandwich for breakfast. "I can't find my hockey socks," I admitted, reaching for the sandwich.

"They're in the wash," Mum said.

What?

"But . . . I didn't ask you to wash them."

Mum turned to me. Her hands were on her hips. That was never a good sign, and it seemed to be happening an awful lot lately. "No, you didn't ask me to, but those socks were practically standing up on their own, begging to be clean."

"But I need them for practice. Today."

"Well, I just put them in the dryer. They're soaking wet."

"But —"

"Why didn't you pack your bag last night?" Dad asked, as he poured a cup of coffee.

Great, they were tag-teaming me, which was something else that seemed to be happening a lot.

"I was doing homework," I told him, knowing that wasn't entirely true.

"No, you were in here," Mum said. "Listening to the radio."

Did she wash the socks to punish me? And if so, what kind of a crazy family did I belong to?

"That was only for a few minutes. Just for the contest."

"The contest?" Mum asked, frowning.

"Hockey trivia," Dad took a sip of his coffee then leaned in to kiss her cheek.

"A contest," Mum sighed. "Here's hoping the grand prize is a passing grade in Math."

"Even better," I told her. "Two tickets to a Canucks game and a chance to shoot from centre ice. For money and prizes."

"Is that right?" Dad asked. "A shot from centre? I thought it was just memorabilia."

"Nope," I told him.

"Rogers Arena, eh? Now that's a prize!"

"Don't encourage him, Gord," Mum warned.

It was kind of a strange thing to say, considering parents were supposed to encourage their kids.

"So, what am I going to do about the socks?" I asked.

"You only have one pair?" Mum asked.

"Yes."

"Why didn't you tell me you needed more?"

"Because I didn't think you were going to steal them right when I needed them," I said, taking a bite of my sandwich. I knew it wasn't the right thing to say as soon as the words were out of my mouth because the temperature in the room dropped about ten degrees.

In two seconds.

Oops.

Mum and Dad both stared at me.

"Sorry. I meant —"

"That you'd like to start taking responsibility for your own laundry?" Mum asked in a tone that would have sounded sweet to anyone who didn't know her.

But I knew her.

"Uh —"

"Or maybe you'd like to pack your own lunches for school?" Dad suggested.

Neither option sounded very good.

"Uh . . . " I wasn't fast enough, and the tag-teaming ended with Mum.

"Or maybe it would be best if you stuck to our original plan and got all of your gear in order the night before practice," she said, one eyebrow raised.

I nodded. "That would be good."

"Yes, it would be," Dad said. "It's always good to have a plan."

Mum dug her keys out of her purse. "In the meantime, you can grab your new socks from the bottom of your chest of drawers."

I started to turn, then stopped in my tracks.

Wait a second.

"I have new socks?"

"Two pairs," she said, like I hadn't just freaked out about not having any. "I bought them at the end of last season."

Man, was she tricky! I spun around to race up the stairs, and remembered halfway up to shout, "Thanks, Mum!"

"Shut up, Nugget!" Wendy shouted from her room.

"J.T." I muttered.

I grabbed my socks, which were still in their packaging, and raced back downstairs to shove them into my hockey bag.

"Ready?" Mum asked as she opened the door for me.

"Yup," I told her, hoisting the huge bag onto my back. The weight almost knocked me over.

"What happened to your hair?" Dad asked.

"Nothing," I said, turning toward the door.

"It has bubbles in it."

The shampoo! "Someone flushed the toilet when I was in the shower," I sighed.

Mum lifted her coffee cup toward her mouth, but not before I heard her chuckle.

"It's not funny."

"You're right," she said, clearing her throat. "I'm the one who flushed it. I'm sorry honey, I just wasn't thinking."

"Good luck at practice," Dad said, then started singing some weird song about tiny bubbles.

I thought he was making it up until Mum started in as well. I scowled at no one in particular as I pulled the door closed behind me. Just as it clicked shut, I heard Wendy yell, "Are you kidding me with the singing? Seriously! I'm trying to sleep!"

Mum was pretty quiet for the first few minutes of the drive, and I hoped she wasn't mad at me.

"Thanks again for getting the socks, Mum," I told her.

"No problem."

I looked out the window and thought for a moment or two. It wasn't like buying me new socks was the only nice thing she'd done for me lately. I'd just finished eating a peanut butter sandwich she got up early to make for me. "And for all the other stuff you do, too," I added.

"It's all part of being a mum," she said, reaching over to give my knee a squeeze.

"Kenny's mum doesn't do all that stuff," I told her.

That's when it hit me.

Kenny!

"Nuts!"

"What?" Mum asked, hitting the brakes.

"Kenny needs a ride to practice!" I couldn't believe I forgot!

"Today?" Mum gasped.

"Yes. Uh, right now."

"Good grief," she groaned, pulling off the road and turning around so we could go back for him. "Why didn't I know anything about this?"

"He only asked me yesterday."

"You're not answering the question," she said, shooting me a look out of the corner of her eye.

"Because I forgot to ask you," I sighed.

"There's been an awful lot of forgetting lately, Jonathan. Please tell me you remembered to do your Math homework."

"I did," I told her, with a nod.

Well, the regular work, anyway. That extra assignment was a stupid idea. Why had I even asked for it? And could I honestly finish it during a fifteen minute recess? If I didn't, would it count as missed homework, or just a missed opportunity to win Mr. Holloway over?

Before I had time to really think about it, we were at Kenny's house. Luckily, the Cavanaughs' kitchen light was on and I could see my buddy standing at the window, waiting for us. I helped him load his bag into the back of the van, and when he climbed in next to me, he looked like someone had glued his eyelids together, too.

"Thanks for the ride, Mrs. McDonald," Kenny said, buckling his seatbelt.

"No problem," she told him, but she caught my eye in the rear-view mirror and I had a feeling she'd have more to say about it later on.

* * *

Practice was insane, and I'm not just saying that because I did a faceplant when we were skating drills and ended up with a bloody nose. I'm saying it because Coach O'Neal told us it was time to start taking the game seriously, and that meant skating hard and fast for what seemed like forever.

I'd thought my workouts during the summer would give me a serious edge over the rest of the guys and they kind of did. But they didn't give me an edge over Coach.

"Let's hustle out there!" he shouted, in between blasts on his whistle.

"I *am* hustling," Colin grunted at me.

"Me too," I grunted back.

"Bayview isn't going to slow down for you guys at next week's game, you know," Coach shouted.

"We know," Colin and I groaned at the same time.

"You've got three days before you face them. Do you want to win?"

"Yes," I heard a couple of guys say.

"What about the rest of you?" Coach shouted.

"Yes," we mumbled.

"I still can't hear you."

"Yes!" we shouted, loud and clear.

For most of practice, I felt like I had too much on my mind to concentrate properly. Life had been kind of a breeze up until twenty-four hours earlier, and it had been going down the tubes ever since, especially on the ice. I should have been a lock for starting right wing, since I'd been on Coach's team forever. Never mind all the extra work I'd done over the summer. That position should have been mine, period.

Eddie Bosko was ruining everything for me.

He was going to be a tough player to beat. He was good, he was strong and he had the size advantage. *And now he was going to be my tutor?* I'd be stuck spending time with him off the ice? That stunk worse than week-old garbage, but there was nothing I could do about it.

And when it came to things I had no control over, there was the fact that I wasn't growing at all. What if I was the size of an eight-year-old when I was seventeen . . . or seventy!

Jeff swiped the puck from me during scrimmage and scored his second goal.

Nuts!

Out of the corner of my eye, I saw Eddie Bosko check Kenny, who tripped over his own skates and wiped out. Eddie did the same thing to Patrick Chen, who was one of the only guys on the team who liked him. Patrick managed to stay on his feet, but barely. In fact, he looked pretty shaken up after Bosko made contact.

That monster was going to help me with Math? He would slowly explain all the calculations that made no sense?

I seriously doubted it, especially when he checked me into the boards three times in four minutes, each hit a little harder than the last.

I didn't give him the satisfaction of seeing it hurt me, though. I grunted, but kept my face totally blank, just like he did. I tried to smirk once, but it probably looked more like a wince, and even with pads on, my elbow felt like it was on fire.

After the last hit, I went after the puck like it was the key to fixing everything that was going wrong. I forgot how tired I was and much pain I'd be in the next morning. I pushed myself as hard as I could, and the people around me even harder.

Unfortunately, that included Kenny, who was rubbing his shoulder and shooting me dirty looks as practice was winding up.

"Geez, Nugget! What's your problem?" he asked, as Coach O'Neal blew his whistle to call us in.

"Sorry, man," I said. "I didn't mean to."

"That doesn't mean it didn't hurt," he said, skating toward centre ice.

"Let's huddle up," Coach said, clapping his hands silently.

I guess he forgot he was wearing gloves.

The group of us skated into a circle and I saw that every one of us was dripping sweat, even Eddie Bosko. That was a good sign, at least. I wiggled my toes, and even they felt sweaty. If my socks stood up on their own from the first practice, the second would have had them dancing around the laundry room.

"I know I ran you guys hard today," Coach O'Neal said, over the sound of us catching our breath. "And you know I did it for your own good."

A couple of the guys nodded.

"We beat Bayview twice last year, but that doesn't mean we can rest on our laurels and —"

"Our what?" Kenny asked.

"Laurels. Don't worry about it right now. Just know that Bayview is hungry for a win. We all know last season left them with something to prove."

"I'll say," Jeff whispered.

Coach shook his head. "But you guys have something to prove too. Being a great team means always looking for ways to get better. That means pushing yourselves, even when you feel like you don't need to."

Coach looked each of us in the eye, one at a time. When it was my turn, I did my best to give him a tough look, by squinting a little.

"Do you need glasses, Nugget?" Colin whispered.

I shook my head and stopped squinting. Apparently my tough look needed some work.

"Okay," Coach said, nodding slowly at his team. "We'll see you Friday morning, bright and early."

Chapter Six

Even though I knew I spent an equal amount of time in each of my classes, it seemed like I was always in Mr. Holloway's room. Even worse, it seemed like I was always three or four steps behind whatever crazy lesson he was teaching in there.

While Mr. Holloway scribbled a bunch of numbers on the board, Carrie Tanaka walked up and down every row, collecting homework assignments. I had a bad feeling as I tried to smooth out the crumpled ball of equations I'd shoved in the bottom of my backpack. I had an even worse feeling knowing I'd spent recess playing street hockey in the school bus parking lot instead of doing my special make-up assignment.

Nuts.

I cringed at the wrinkled assignment I had completed. When I'd worked on it the night before, it seemed like getting half the answers right would be good enough. But if it was half right, it was also half wrong. Now *that* was the kind of depressing Math I could calculate.

Another calculation?

The chance of Mr. Holloway giving me another make-up assignment was about zero percent.

So, there was only one thing I could do, and that was to use the next two minutes to try saving myself. I opened my textbook to the right page and tore some loose-leaf paper from my binder. Where was my pencil? I dug through the front pocket of my bag until I found it, but by then Carrie Tanaka was only two rows away. Two stinkin' rows!

I had to work fast!

I licked my lips, which were suddenly dry, and read over the first question.

Surprise, surprise. It didn't make sense. (To me, anyway.)

I read it again as Carrie turned into the row next to mine. The longer I stared, the more the numbers and letters started to look like the pictures of hieroglyphics we'd seen in Mr. Marshall's class. Hieroglyphics it would take an archaeologist years to decipher.

And I was no archaeologist.

"Mr. McDonald," Mr. Holloway said, making me jump in my seat. "You appear to be racing ahead of the rest of the class."

Racing ahead? I was trying to catch up!

"No, I —" I gulped. *Please don't make me write on the board.*

"I have yet to instruct you or anyone else to open their textbooks, and there you are, feverishly working."

"I —"

"And if you aren't racing ahead," he said, peering at me over the top of his glasses, "I certainly hope you aren't trying to finish up an earlier assignment."

"No, I —"

"Class, where is homework meant to be done?"

"At home," almost everyone said at the same time, like a bunch of robots.

Even I whispered along, since he'd been training us since the first day of class.

He nodded and started walking down the aisle toward me. "Not in class, not at recess, not on the bus, or in the back seat of the family minivan."

Had he been spying on me all year?

Carrie Tanaka gave me a sympathetic look and I handed over the crumpled assignment. She reached for the page I had just started scribbling on.

I held on to it and shook my head as Mr. Holloway continued, "Not in the minutes before class, and certainly not once class has begun." He stood next to my desk. "Am I making myself clear, Mr. McDonald?"

"Yes," I told him.

He glanced at the open page of my textbook and raised one eyebrow at me, just like Mum. "I don't imagine I'm going to discover your make-up assignment among the sheets Miss Tanaka has just collected."

I shook my head slowly instead of saying anything.

"Is that a negative, Mr. McDonald?"

"Yes . . . I mean, no," I babbled. "I mean no, you will not find it."

"It being the assignment that you requested to compensate for yet another uncompleted assignment?"

"Yes," I told him, my voice barely a squeak.

Mr. Holloway sighed and started walking back toward the chalkboard.

Whew.

At least he hadn't made me go to the front of the class.

"Mr. McDonald?" he said, suddenly spinning around to face me.

"Yes?" I gulped.

"Please join me at the front of the class."

Nuts!

Travis Cosgrove and Jason Kiniski both snickered as I shuffled past them on the way to certain doom.

"You can do it," Kenny whispered.

Of course, he was worse than me at Math and was probably just relieved he wasn't Mr. Holloway's target.

When I stood at the board and faced the class, the thirty faces I'd known forever looked more like two hundred strangers. They were all staring at me and waiting for me to mess up. I didn't have much time to think about it though, because Mr. Holloway was already throwing a bunch of numbers at me. I tried to follow the story of some friends stopping at a vending machine to buy a bunch of sandwiches. I'd seen vending machine sandwiches on the ferry, and I wouldn't have paid a nickel for squished ham or dried out turkey.

But of course, that wasn't the question.

What was the question? Something about a $20 bill and some change. Did he say 5 guys and 3 sandwiches? No, 6 sandwiches. My brain was like a tornado, swirling around in my skull. The room was totally silent. I wanted to count on my fingers, but I couldn't decide whether my thumb represented a sandwich or a person.

Why couldn't he ask me a *hockey* question?

"We're all waiting, Mr. McDonald."

Did he think I didn't know that? I would have rather been just about anywhere, even squished by a sumo wrestler or slammed into the boards by Eddie Bosko. I glanced at my enemy, and he just stared blankly at me, the way he had before, like he had no idea who I was. Like he hadn't spent that very morning trying to destroy me on the ice.

Jerk.

I turned to face the board again, and that was when I heard Eddie Bosko.

"Two-fifty," he said, in that deep Dad-voice.

"Mr. Bosko, you have something to contribute?" Mr. Holloway said, frowning.

Eddie sighed. "The 6 sandwiches at $3.75 apiece will cost $22.50. The one guy can put in his 20 and the other 4 have to come up with the remaining $2.50. That's the *answer*."

Mr. Holloway looked like he'd just eaten something very sour. "And the *question* wasn't directed toward you."

Eddie Bosko shrugged and I half-expected him to ask, "So what are you gonna do about it?"

I stood at the board like a big dork, gripping my piece of chalk and waiting for someone to tell me what to do.

Mr. Holloway cleared his throat. "Take your seat, Mr. McDonald."

I made it back to my desk in about two seconds flat, trying to figure out if Eddie Bosko had saved or humiliated me. As much as it shocked me, I was leaning toward saved.

For the rest of the class, I tried really hard to understand the problems Mr. Holloway worked through on the board and I tried even harder to understand why Eddie Bosko would help me.

* * *

When the bell rang, I grabbed my books and raced into the hallway to catch up with him. He was at least a foot taller than the rest of the kids, so he was easy to follow. When he stopped at the drinking fountain, I waited for him to finish slurping and stand up straight. When he did, I kind of waved at him, then felt like an idiot and shoved my hand in my pocket.

He wiped his mouth with his sleeve and stared at me.

"I just wanted to say thanks for helping me in there," I said, keeping my voice steady.

He didn't say anything for about ten seconds, which felt like ten years.

I tried to smile.

He sighed, then said, "I got tired of watching you stand there with your mouth hanging open, like a flounder on the line, right before it gets nailed with a bat."

"Oh," I said, feeling my face turn red.

"It was kind of pathetic," he said, then turned toward the cafeteria.

"Eddie?" I called after him.

"Yeah?" he asked, over his shoulder. He didn't even bother turning around.

"You're going to be my tutor, you know." My cheeks were so hot they felt sunburned. "I need help with Math."

He stopped and turned to stare at me again, long and hard.

"No kidding," he said, then walked away.

* * *

Thankfully, my day got better in gym period, since Mrs. Ramsey let us play floor hockey. Five of the guys from the Cougars were in my class, and four of us ended up on one team, which meant trouble for the competition, especially the girls.

Hannah Richards and Molly Irving stood around,

twirling their hair and gossiping for almost the whole game. They only stopped talking long enough to scream whenever the bright orange puck whizzed past them at 500 kilometres per hour, which happened at least twenty times. The rest of the girls were pretty useless, too. I knew a bunch of them were good skaters, since I'd seen the Cutter Bay Ice Dancers practise at the rink, but skating was only one part of playing hockey and they sure were lame on the gym floor.

Why anyone would waste their ice time spinning around in a sparkly jumpsuit, flapping their arms and smiling, was a mystery to me.

"I'm open!" Justin shouted from right in front of the net.

He was always open, because he stunk.

Patrick passed me the puck and I took off down the floor.

"I'm open," Justin shouted again.

If he kept announcing it, he wouldn't be open for long.

"Nugget, down here!" he called to me.

Yeesh.

I flicked the puck past Tamara, who barely even moved to intercept it, and it landed right at Justin's feet. He took a huge swing at it, like he was playing *golf*, and missed the puck completely. I lifted my stick and ran down the gym floor, watching in shock as Justin missed it again. The other kids were swarming like bees, and I only had a couple of seconds before someone was sure to steal the puck. I whipped in behind Justin, kind of like Eddie Bosko had done to me at that first practice, and took possession.

"Way to go, Nugget!" Kenny shouted.

J.T. was looking like more of a lost cause by the minute. I tapped the puck to the left, deked James Kwan out, then zipped past Sean. There it was. The goal was tended by Erica Brioche, whose eyes were closed so tight she probably could have seen out of the back of her head. I could have made a big, dramatic goal, but I felt sorry for her. After all, she couldn't help the fact that she was a girl.

Instead of whaling on it, I just nudged the puck past her for an easy point and my whole team cheered. It felt awesome!

After twenty minutes and fourteen more goals (five scored by me), Mrs. Ramsey blew the whistle to end the game.

I wished I could have played all day.

Me and the guys got changed in the locker room, high-fiving and cheering over our victory, then split up to go to our next classes.

I was already counting the hours until Big Danny Donlin's radio show. I'd packed *Shoot! Third Edition* in my bag, and I peeked at it during Social Studies and French. Practise makes perfect, and what could be more perfect than a shot from centre ice? Nothing.

At lunch, I sat with Kenny and Colin and, as usual, I swapped my homemade oatmeal raisin cookies for Kenny's Twinkie. Mum would have screamed if she'd seen me take the first big, bad bite.

"So, we're two practices into the season. What do you guys think of Bosko now?" Colin asked.

Kenny glanced at me before answering, "He's still a jerk."

"A big jerk," I added.

"But he can play," Colin said, through a mouthful of his turkey sandwich. His Mum always made it with cranberry sauce, which was gross.

"Sure, he's good," I told him. "But he's still a jerk."

"Even at school," Kenny said, shaking his head. "I said hi to him yesterday and he just kept walking."

"I tried to be nice, too," I told the guys. "But he just stares back."

"Maybe something's wrong with him," Colin suggested. "Maybe he's really dumb."

I thought about whether I should spill the beans and decided it was better for them to hear it from me than someone else. "He's actually a genius," I sighed. "Well, in Math, anyway. He's kind of going to be my tutor."

"No way!" Kenny gasped.

"Yes way," I told him. "Starting tomorrow."

"But you don't need a tutor."

"Not as much as you do, Kenny."

"Thanks a lot," he said, elbowing me.

"Mum knows I'm having trouble with Math, so —"

"That's brutal," Colin said, his sandwich halfway to his mouth. "Your Mum must be pure evil."

"Dude, she makes him eat multigrain bread," Kenny told him. "She's vicious." He quickly glanced at me. "Sorry, Nugget. You know what I mean, though, right? She can be —"

"Actually, I like multi—" I started, but Colin cut me off.

"Tutored by the guy who wants to steal your position," he said, shaking his head. "I can't believe it."

The truth was, I could hardly believe it myself.

Chapter Seven

After school, I walked home with Kenny but didn't waste any time yakking on the corner, since I had work to do. The Red Wings game would be on at seven, so I only had a couple of hours before dinner to study for the trivia contest at eight and get my homework done. It was going to be tight.

After what he said at the water fountain, I'd decided that if Eddie Bosko wanted to be a jerk about my Math skills (okay, lack of Math skills), there was no reason I should give him extra ammo. And that meant trying to figure out as much Math as I could before the first tutoring session, which was scheduled for the very next day.

I poured myself a glass of milk and grabbed a couple of carob brownies from the Tupperware snack tub before heading upstairs to my room.

Trivia, then Math?

I sighed.

Nope. Math, then trivia.

Of course, I wanted to be ready for Big Danny Donlin's question of the night, but even I knew Math was more important right then, so I focused. And focusing meant I worked so hard and for so long on number crunching that I thought brain sweat was going to start leaking out of my ears.

It took me an hour to get through the first page of the Math assignment and my gut feeling was that I only had about half of the answers right again.

Nuts.

I took a break to go downstairs and refill my milk glass, figuring my brain could probably use the protein.

Back in my room, I turned to the second page and got to work. I wasn't sure when Math had started to get so hard for me, but I wished I'd been paying attention when it did. Most of the other kids understood it, but I'd always been too busy thinking about other stuff in class. Like hockey.

I started to reach for *Shoot! Third Edition*, but stopped myself. I had to stick with Math.

Me and what was left of my melting brain were super relieved when Mum called us for dinner.

"Awfully quiet up there," Dad said, handing me a bunch of cutlery so I could set the table.

"Homework," I said, with a shrug.

"They're really piling it on this year, eh?" he asked, grabbing some napkins and following me into the dining room.

"Kind of." I scooted around the table, putting knives and forks in place while Mum and Wendy brought dinner out from the kitchen.

Mum had made meatloaf, and even though that's the kind of thing most kids hate, hers was awesome.

"Mum," I told her, in between mouthfuls, "this is so good they could serve it in the school cafeteria."

"Is that supposed to be a compliment?" Wendy asked.

"Uh-huh."

"Jonathan," Mum said, raising her eyebrow.

Great, the language police were on duty. When did my dinner table turn into Mr. Holloway's class?

"Sorry, I meant yes."

Mum smiled and reached over to mess up my hair. "I'm glad you like it, honey."

"I was hoping for chicken or something," Wendy sighed. She hated meatloaf, but I was pretty sure it had more to do with the name than the taste.

Meat. *Loaf.*

She was picky like that. She hated Guy LaCroix from the Leafs, just because she couldn't pronounce his name right. And he was an amazing hockey player! She wouldn't touch the milk if she saw me drink from the carton. She wouldn't let me have the front seat in Mum's van. Ever. She wouldn't say hi to me in public.

After the day I'd had, I was in no mood to deal with my big, moody sister. I squirted more ketchup onto my plate and dipped a juicy hunk of meatloaf into it.

"Ugh. How gross is that?" Wendy asked.

I thought about the time I'd walked into the living room and caught her by surprise.

"Less gross than swapping spit with Scott Cody," I told her.

Wendy dropped her fork with a clang. "What?"

"Or maybe it's Scott Cootie?" That was a good one! And I'd thought of it on the spot. I couldn't wait to tell Kenny.

"Jonathan," Dad warned.

"What?" I shrugged. "Meatloaf is way less gross."

"You are such a twerp," Wendy sneered.

"Just because I play ice hockey and you play tongue hockey?" Yes! Another zinger!

She gasped, then just sat there with her mouth hanging open.

If Eddie Bosko had seen her, he would have thought looking like flounders ran in my family.

"Are you going to let him get away with this?" Wendy asked, looking first at Mum, then Dad. Her braces were clogged with bits of green beans. Now *that* was gross, but I knew better than to point it out.

"Everyone just settle down and enjoy the meal," Dad said.

"Did you even hear what he said?" Wendy asked. Her eyes were all bugged out and her face was bright red.

"Jonathan, I think you owe your sister an apology," Mum said.

"For what?" I asked.

"Uh, being born?" Wendy snapped.

"Wendy," Mum warned.

"What, he can say whatever he wants and I can't?"

"These potatoes are fantastic," Dad said, passing Wendy the bowl. "Didn't Mum do a great job with dinner?"

Wendy ignored the bowl. "I can't eat another bite until he apologizes."

Mum and Dad both looked at me.

"Sorry," I finally said. "Can you pass the beans?"

"That's it?" Wendy asked.

I thought about it for a second. "And the pepper, please."

"I meant your apology," my sister growled.

"You can do better, Nugget," Mum told me.

"J.T.," I reminded her, then turned toward Wendy and put on my most sincere expression, "Wendy, I'm sorry you sucked face with Scott Cody."

"That's it!" she shouted, shoving her seat back and standing up. "I'm not putting up with this."

"Wendy, have a seat," Mum said.

"Forget it," she said, stomping upstairs like a typical teenage drama queen. When she slammed her bedroom door, the table was totally silent.

I started to take another bite of meatloaf, but stopped when I saw Mum staring at me.

Uh-oh.

"What on earth did you do that for?" she asked.

"What?"

"You know perfectly well what," Dad said.

"I don't know," I sighed. The truth was, part of me wanted to take my rotten day out on someone else, and Wendy was the closest target. Of course, I knew Mum and Dad wouldn't understand that kind of explanation, since they thought being eleven was easy.

Ha!

"Well, as soon as you're finished with dinner, you're going straight to your room."

I checked the clock and saw that it was 6:37.

"Until the game starts?" I asked.

Mum actually snorted with laughter. "You aren't watching the game tonight."

"What?" I couldn't believe what I was hearing!

"After what you just pulled with your sister, there's no way you're watching hockey."

All of the air left my body. She had to be kidding.

"But . . . but it's the Red Wings."

"And then it's the Oilers, the Rangers, the Bruins," Mum said, counting them off on her fingers. "That's not the point."

She had the schedule all messed up, but that wasn't the point either. I looked toward my only hope, but Dad was shaking his head. "I'm with Mum on this one."

"Are you kidding me?" I gasped. It was the Red Wings!

"Finish your dinner before it gets cold," Mum said.

All of a sudden, I wasn't hungry. Not even for meatloaf. I pushed my food around on my plate for a few minutes, trying to make it look like I was eating something, but I wasn't fooling anyone.

Mum and Dad chatted about their busy days at work, as if they hadn't just destroyed my life. Well, my evening, anyway.

"May I be excused?" I asked, when I couldn't stand it anymore.

"Yes," Mum said. "And please clear your sister's place, as well as yours."

I carried the dishes into the kitchen, then rinsed them and loaded the dishwasher. When I passed the table again on the way to my prison cell, Dad said, "Be sure to offer your sister a real apology on your way up."

"I will," I mumbled.

I climbed the stairs and stopped at the top for a second or two before knocking on Wendy's door. I could hear music, so I knocked louder.

"What?"

I cleared my throat. "I'm sorry," I said, through the door.

"Go away," she growled.

So I did. I went to my room and flopped on the bed with my textbooks piled around me. I didn't feel like doing anything, especially homework. I flipped through my Math assignment again, then opened *Over the Moon* and started reading.

Before I knew it, almost an hour and a half had flown

by, and that seemed crazier than the rest of my day put together. I couldn't believe it. I'd never been "lost" in a book before, but I actually liked reading it. Mrs. Foster would probably collapse when she found out I'd read ahead.

I glanced at the clock.

Almost eight!

Big Danny Donlin was coming on!

I jumped off the bed and ran downstairs, where I could hear the game on in the living room. It was like a gigantic magnet was on the other side of the wall, trying to pull me in, but I couldn't watch. When Mum and Dad said no, they really meant it. I froze for a second, trying to hear the score at least, but Dad had it turned down too low.

Nuts!

I hurried into the kitchen and climbed on the stool to reach the radio. I hit the power button, then had to scramble to turn the volume down. I rolled the dial through mini blasts of news and music until I was on PUCK Radio.

My whole body was tense.

The radio station was broadcasting the game!

Of course, Mum and Dad hadn't said anything about not being allowed to *listen* to it, but I was pretty sure that was a no-no. Even tuning in for the contest was pushing my luck.

"And now that we've got a commercial break in the game," Big Danny Donlin said, practically into my ear, "let's get to tonight's question."

"Yes," I whispered.

"For a signed copy of Kenny McElroy's *NHL History*, we are looking for caller number seven to tell us which team drafted Brett Hull."

First Bobby Hull, now Brett?

This time, I knew the answer, right away. I'd read it in *Shoot! Third Edition* during Social Studies!

The Calgary Flames.

It was only a second or two before a call came in. Man, if people were dialing that fast, I was going to have to start practising punching in the station's number so I'd be ready on the big day.

"Who's on the line?" Big Danny Donlin asked.

"Chris from Comox."

"Hello Chris from Comox. Do you have an answer for me?"

"The Calgary Flames," I whispered.

"Yeah, I do. It was the Blues."

"Ouch," Big Danny Donlin groaned. "No it wasn't. Next caller?"

A woman's voice said, "This is Fran from Parksville."

"And the answer is?"

"The Calgary Flames?" she asked.

"You've got it!" said Big Danny Donlin.

I clicked the radio off with a smile, happy I had it right.

With Dad's help the night before, I was two-for-two. A hundred percent, if I felt like putting a Math spin on it. I could practically hear myself winning the contest. I could hear the crowd cheering as I moved to centre ice. I could hear my heart pounding as I lined up my shot.

I could hear Mum asking Dad if he wanted anything from the kitchen!

I jumped to the floor, as quiet as a cat, and pushed the stool back into place.

I tiptoed past the den and ran upstairs as quickly and quietly as I could. And when I was safely behind my closed door, I moved *Shoot! Third Edition* to my bedside table and made myself open my Math textbook.

Chapter Eight

I woke up the next morning at five o'clock and was halfway out of the bed, my toes curling from the cold, when I realized it was Thursday.

That meant no practice, which stunk.

I slipped my nearly frozen foot back under the covers. Sleeping in, on the other hand? That didn't stink a bit. I pulled the blankets tight around me and rolled toward the wall to fall back asleep. Maybe I could finish my dream about skating circles around Eddie Bosko. I'd woken up just as it was getting really good. I closed my eyes and imagined coming to a quick stop and spraying ice in his face. Perfect.

What seemed like three seconds after I fell asleep, Mom was knocking on my door.

"Time for school," she said.

Already? Sure enough, when I rubbed my eyes and looked at the glowing red lights of my alarm clock, I saw that it was already seven.

Nuts!

I'd slept for two whole hours and it felt like I'd barely blinked. I rolled out of bed with a groan and tripped over a pile of dirty laundry that must have sprouted up overnight.

Sprouted.

I rubbed my eyes, thinking of sprouts as I stared at the pile by my feet. If dirty clothes sat for long enough, could something actually grow on them? I frowned.

Kenny swore the running shoes he'd left soaking wet on his back steps last spring had *mushrooms* on the laces. How gross was that? Gross enough to make me pick up the pile and dump it into the laundry hamper, figuring I was better safe than sorry.

I left my pyjamas on the bathroom counter and climbed into the shower. Just as I was getting the shampoo out of my hair, I heard the toilet flush again. I wasn't fast enough to get out of the spray and I got scorched, right on my ribs.

"Yowch!" I gasped, squishing myself into the tiled corner to escape from the steaming water.

I was going to have to talk to Mum about this. I waited a few seconds and dipped my fingers under the spray. Whew. Back to the right temperature. I moved back into position and the toilet flushed again.

Nuts!

This time, the scalding water got my shoulders.

"Urgh!" I grunted, cramming into the corner again to wait it out.

When it cooled down, I tried again. Another flush.

"Come *on*," I shrieked.

Shampoo dripped into my eyes and they stung like crazy. I rubbed them with the backs of my hands while I was squished in the corner, but that only made the stinging worse. When I reached out to check the temperature, the water was still way too hot. I couldn't reach the showerhead to turn the spray away from me, so the only choice was to turn it off at the tap.

Great. Dad would be singing the tiny bubble song again.

I was totally ticked off and I practically ripped the shower curtain open, trying to find a towel to wrap around my waist. It hurt to open my eyes and when I did, I could only squint, but that was enough.

Standing next to the toilet, fully dressed, with her book bag on her shoulder and a glare just for me, was Wendy.

"Too bad. I was ready for another flush," she said, letting go of the handle.

"That was you every . . . I got totally . . . what did you do that for?"

She smiled. "Payback."

"For what?" I asked, trying to wipe the shampoo out of my eyes again.

"Are you kidding me?" she asked, jaw dropping open.

I stared at her with one eye. The other one was too busy oozing shampoo to shoot her a dirty look. "Never mind," I said.

"*That's* your apology?"

"What? You're the one who blinded me!"

"And you're the one who told Mum and Dad about me and Scott."

"But it was true."

"It was last year, Nugget, and they didn't need to know about it."

"But —"

"Just like they don't need to know that you were creeping around in the kitchen last night."

Nuts!

"Fine," I said.

She looked at me for a few seconds, waiting for more. But more what?

"Fine," I said again. She'd made her point.

My sister rolled her eyes. "Okay, that's not an apology either."

"I'm sorry, Wendy," I said, as sincerely as I could while goose bumps popped up all over my body.

"Apology accepted," she grunted, turning to walk out of the washroom. She was a dangerous one, that was for sure.

I waited until I knew she was downstairs before I turned the water back on. By that time, Mum had the dishwasher or something running, so my shower was only lukewarm.

It wasn't a great start to the day, and my tutoring session with Eddie Bosko meant it probably wouldn't end well, either.

* * *

When I was finally dressed, I trudged into the kitchen, wishing I'd had practice that morning so I could have taken all my frustrations out on the ice.

I sat at my usual spot and spread butter on the blueberry waffle that was waiting for me, before loading it up with syrup. As soon as I tasted the first mouthful, I felt a bit better. After all, how bad could life be if something that awesome was just sitting there, ready to be eaten. I cut off another bite and ran it through a puddle of syrup before shoving it into my mouth.

Mmmm . . . syrup.

My hero Jean Ducette's family was in the maple syrup business, and that made me love it even more than I already did. He was from a tiny town in Quebec, where his family had lived for over a hundred years. A whole century!

He had eleven brothers and sisters, and the kids used to be called the Ducette Dozen.

When he was growing up, the whole family worked to collect sap in the spring. They had these things called sugar shacks where they boiled it to make syrup. They had a big party while they worked and even poured maple syrup on ice to eat for a treat!

Yum city.

When Jean grew up, he was an awesome hockey player and he had to decide between the NHL and the syrup business.

I knew what I'd pick, and it involved a puck. Lucky for me (and the Canucks), he picked hockey, along with three of his brothers, and all four of them became professional players! Their dad had to be the proudest guy on the whole planet. In fact, he was so proud, he made limited edition maple syrup bottles shaped like each of the boys, and sold them at Christmas.

I talked Mum into buying me the Jean Ducette bottle at Safeway one day. Even though the syrup is probably awesome, I'll never open it. It's way too valuable to eat.

I took a bite of my waffle and closed my eyes while I chewed. My mum was the absolute best cook on the island. I took another bite. Make that the planet.

"Good?" she asked, drying her hands with a tea towel.

My mouth was full, so I gave her a thumbs up.

"I'm glad," she said, with a laugh. "I'll make some cookies for you and Eddie to munch on this afternoon."

I stopped chewing. Eddie Bosko probably ate cast iron, not cookies.

"He'll be here at three-thirty," she added.

I almost choked. "Here?" I gasped, through the waffle.

Mum looked at me like I was crazy. "Of course, here. You guys are going to be studying together."

I swallowed hard. "But here?"

I thought we'd meet at the school library or something. It was bad enough that he was in my locker room and my classroom. Did he really have to be in my living room too? Or my bedroom?

I didn't want him to come over and see the "cute" framed photos of me at every age as he climbed the stairs. I didn't want him to give Mum and Dad the same blank stare he gave me all the time. I didn't want him to watch Wendy make fun of me.

I didn't want him in my house at all!

It was totally crazy.

Batman didn't invite the Joker to his bat cave. Superman didn't have Lex Luthor over for Sunday dinner. There was no reason the gorilla should even knock on my door, let alone walk through it.

"Are you feeling okay, honey?" Mum asked, reaching over to lay her hand on my forehead.

Aha! Maybe that was my ticket to freedom! If I told her I was sick, I could stay home from school and Eddie Bosko could stay out of my life, at least for a day.

But when I glanced at Mum, I knew I was kidding myself. She'd have the tutoring rescheduled so fast, my head would spin.

"I'm fine," I told her. I dug into the rest of my waffle, but it had kind of lost its flavour.

Great.

Eddie Bosko had actually stripped the taste out of blueberry waffles, without even trying.

* * *

I met Kenny outside for the walk to school in drizzling rain. We pulled up our hoods, since only girls carry umbrellas.

"That game was awesome," Kenny said.

"What game?" I asked, still distracted by thoughts of Eddie Bosko.

"Duh, Nugget. The Red Wings last night? We destroyed you!"

"Oh," I sighed. "I didn't get to watch."

Kenny turned to stare at me. "What do you mean?"

"I had to spend the whole night in my room, doing homework."

"Why?"

"I was mean to my sister."

"Did you kill her?"

It was my turn to stare. "No! Are you crazy?"

He shrugged. "Well, that's the only thing I can think of that's bad enough to miss the game."

"We just had a fight at dinner."

"A fistfight?"

"What's wrong with you? She's a girl, Kenny."

He shrugged again.

"Look, I was rude to her, okay?"

"And you missed the whole game for that?"

"Yeah."

"For being rude? Man, I wish my brother lived at your place." He shook his head. "He'd be grounded forever. Did you at least get to listen to PUCK?"

"Yeah, I snuck downstairs for the trivia question."

"I didn't get it."

"I did," I said, proud of myself.

"Cool. Did you try calling in?"

"Nope."

"Why not?"

"I'm waiting for the last day. I want to win the game tickets."

"And the shot from centre ice," Kenny said, nodding.

"Of course."

"You know, everyone's going to be trying for that, Nugget."

"J.T.," I said automatically, then shrugged. "Somebody has to win. Why not me?"

Kenny was quiet for a few seconds. "I guess you're right."

He didn't sound very sure, but I decided to believe him anyway. The way things had been going, it could be the only time I was right all week.

* * *

My day went pretty smoothly, especially English class. For the first time that year, I was the kid with a hand up to answer questions, and I even asked two of my own. Mrs. Foster looked like she might fall over from shock when she realized I'd actually been reading *Over the Moon*. Star of the class Annie McHale stared at me like I was from outer space.

"I didn't even know you could read," she whispered.

"Thanks a lot," I whispered back.

When it was time for Social Studies, I did okay there, too. Mr. Marshall didn't call on me, but I knew the answers to four of his questions, anyway. It was a good thing I'd cracked the Socials book after Math the night before.

Apparently, studying worked.

At lunch me and the guys ate as fast as we could, then headed to the gym to play a little pickup game. My team won by a landslide, and after all of the rotten stuff that had been happening, it seemed like things were finally going my way.

Of course, knowing Eddie Bosko was coming over still drove me nuts, but after a good day at school, I felt like I could handle it, and handle him. When I really thought about it, I knew he was just a kid my own age, who happened to be good at hockey and Math.

What was the big deal?

"What's the big deal?" Kenny asked on the walk home. "The big deal is that he's a huge jerk, trying to steal your place on the Cougars."

"And I'll do my best to defend it," I told him.

"Oh, man," he said, slapping his forehead. "We're talking about a kid who can bench press 150!"

One fifty! "Who told you that?"

"Omar."

"And how does Omar know?" I asked.

Kenny frowned. "I think Jeff told him."

"And how does Jeff know?"

"I'm not sure."

"Look, Eddie Bosko might be big and he might be strong, but he's still an eleven-year-old."

"Who shaves," Kenny added.

"He does not," I said, rolling my eyes. From what I could tell, Bosko was keeping the mustache.

"Well, you're either brave or stupid, having him over to your place."

"Thanks, Kenny."

"Now the guy is going to know your weak spot."

"Math?" I snorted. "He's in our class, Kenny. It's not exactly a secret."

And that's when it hit me. *Everyone* had a weakness.

Mine was Math, Kenny's was spiders (and common sense), Mum's was chocolate, Dad's was computers, and Wendy's was Scott Cody.

Even Superman had a weakness, so that got me wondering.

What was Eddie Bosko's kryptonite?

Chapter Nine

I lay on my bed, flipping through the pages of *Shoot! Third Edition* and waiting for Eddie Bosko to show up and destroy my afternoon. When the doorbell rang, I shut the book, closed my eyes for a second and took a deep breath before standing up.

I stopped at the top of the stairs and saw that Mum had already let the gorilla into the house. She was actually smiling as she took Eddie's jacket, like he was a normal person. Like he was welcome.

"Hey," I said, hurrying down the stairs.

The sooner Mum was out of the way, the less possible embarrassment I'd have to deal with.

"It's so nice of you to come over and help Nugget," she said, slipping the jacket onto a hanger.

"J.T.," I sighed.

Mum winced. "Sorry, honey. I'm working on it."

"Nugget?" Eddie asked, raising an eyebrow and looking at me.

He hadn't heard the rest of the team calling me that?

Maybe he never listened. "I was trying to get J.T. going, but —"

His eyebrow didn't move.

"Nugget works, I guess," I said, shrugging.

That was the moment I totally gave up on trying to change my name. I was Nugget McDonald, whether I liked it or not, and I'd just have to accept it.

"I'll grab some cookies and I'll leave you boys to it," Mum said, disappearing into the kitchen.

"Cookies?" the gorilla asked.

Both of the eyebrows were raised. I couldn't tell if he was making fun of the idea or not, so I pretended I didn't hear him.

"We can sit over here, I guess," I said, tilting my head toward the dining room table.

"Why don't we just go to your room?" Eddie Bosko asked.

Because I'd rather die? "Mine? I, uh . . . it's kind of a mess," I stammered.

"A mess," he repeated, with that blank stare I hated.

"Yeah, a mess. As in messy."

The big Math genius sure had his problems with English. He wasn't going to see any more of my personal life than he had to. I'd already decided this was business. Math business, and nothing more.

I pulled out a chair and sat down.

After a few seconds, Eddie Bosko did the same, right across from me.

He stared.

I stared back.

He still stared.

"So?" I finally asked.

"Where are your books?"

Nuts!

I'd left them in my room.

I ran upstairs to get them, and when I returned, Eddie Bosko smirked at me. We were off to a great start.

"Here we go," Mum said, carrying a tray with two tall glasses of milk and a plate of peanut butter cookies in from the kitchen.

"Thanks, Mum," I said, hoping she'd make a fast exit.

I breathed a sigh of relief when she wiped her hands on her apron and left the room.

Eddie looked the cookies over.

"You're not allergic to peanuts, are you?" I asked, hopefully. Maybe that was his kryptonite!

"No," he said, reaching for two of them.

Nuts.

"Are you allergic to anything?" I asked.

"Am I what?" He stared at me like I was a flounder again. "No." He grabbed two more, as if the word "sharing" wasn't even in his vocabulary.

Jerk.

"Not even dogs or penicillin or something?"

"No." He opened his textbook and started flipping through the pages, like he was already bored.

I cleared my throat, ready to dig deeper. "You know what I hate?" I asked.

"Math," he said, without looking up.

"No, well, yeah, but snakes, too."

The blank stare was back.

"What about you?" I asked.

He paused. "What about me?"

"Do you hate snakes or . . . anything?"

He was silent for about thirty seconds while I felt my armpits getting sweaty. His stare-down was worse than Mum's, and that was saying something.

When I couldn't take it anymore, I tried again. "Spiders? Or clowns —" I stopped myself.

Clowns? Man, I was getting desperate.

"You don't hate anything?" I asked.

"Yeah, there's something I hate," Bosko finally said.

"Really?" I practically shrieked.

"Questions," he said.

I cleared my throat, awkwardly. "Oh."

"Look, do you want to learn Math or not?" he asked, checking his watch. "I get paid by the hour, so it doesn't matter to me."

What? Mum was *paying* him? Just when I thought the situation couldn't get any more embarrassing, there it was.

"I guess so," I told him, wishing I was anywhere else on the planet, and that included Mr. Holloway's classroom.

"Because I've got other stuff I could be doing right now, like working on my slapshot."

That got my attention.

If getting paid to help me meant that he wasn't practising, it was money well spent, wasn't it? Except that I wasn't practising either. Working on his slapshot, eh? Had he just revealed his weakness? That would be very convenient, because my slapshot just happened to be . . . awesome.

"Okay," he sighed. "Let's get started."

"Sure." I opened my textbook and glanced over to see what page he was on.

"What's your problem?" Eddie asked.

All I did was look at him! My face felt hot again. "My, uh . . . I don't have a problem."

He sighed with what I knew from living with Wendy was exasperation. "With *Math*, I mean. What don't you get?"

Oh, that problem. How was I supposed to sum it up? I didn't get what Mr. Holloway wrote on the board. I didn't get the homework. I didn't get —

"Fractions? Percentages?" he asked.

Yes and yes.

"Word problems are pretty hard, I guess," I finally said. They were the most confusing, anyway.

"Not really, but okay. We'll start there." Eddie flipped further into his book and told me to turn to page seventy-eight.

"Read over problem number one first," he said.

"Jane and Susan are —"

"Not out loud."

"Oh, right," I mumbled, then read the most confusing sentence of my life. Who was Susan, and why weren't she and Jane travelling together?

"So?" he asked, when I was done.

"I don't even know where St. Hubert is," I told him.

Eddie Bosko shook his head. "It doesn't matter."

"But —" I pointed to the question.

"None of it matters. This isn't a Geography test. All we care about are the numbers."

"But —"

"How many people are we talking about?"

Susan and Jane. "Two."

He nodded. "And how many different distances?"

I read the question over again: 400 kilometres, 70 kilometres, and 210 kilometres. "Three."

"Then that's all we need to concentrate on. Get it?"

"I guess," I lied. That seemed way too simple.

"The rest of it, like the names and all that? They're only there to confuse you."

What was the point of that? Wasn't Math confusing enough already?

"Okay?" he asked.

"Yeah," I said, but I wasn't so sure.

Eddie sat forward in his seat and stared.

Now what?

"So, what do we care about?" he asked.

Surviving the afternoon. "Numbers?" I asked.

"Yeah." He actually smiled (not wide enough to show the fangs I was sure were there, but it was something) and reached across the table to punch me lightly on the arm. "*Numbers.*"

Whew.

We worked through the problem together and when we got the answer, it kind of made sense. Kind of.

"Okay, next one," Eddie said, pointing to the second word problem.

I read it, but was confused about whether we were supposed to be figuring out how far Winnipeg was from Moose Jaw, or how long it would take to get there.

"Get started," Eddie said.

"I'm, uh . . . not sure where to —"

The cold stare was back, this time with a groan. "We did one just like this, two seconds ago."

"I know, but it's different information and —"

"It doesn't matter," he growled. "We only care about the numbers. Weren't you paying attention?"

"Yeah, but —"

"Why don't you get it?"

Was he kidding me? Did he honestly think figuring out

one measly problem was going to solve everything?

"Nugget," he sneered.

"Look," I growled back. "It's not like I'm going to master it in one stinking try. It's going to take practise." I thought of his kryptonite. "Just like you have to practise your slapshot."

Eddie Bosko looked like me might punch me, but he spoke instead. "My slapshot kills. It's the most accurate in the league, okay?"

Nuts. Not what I wanted to hear.

"Fine," I muttered.

"Pretty soon, no one's going to be able to stop it."

"Great." I shrugged like it didn't matter, but it did.

"Because I'm working on speed. Every afternoon, from five until six, I whale on a puck in the backyard."

"Good for you," I grunted.

"Now, do you want to figure out this problem or not? It doesn't matter to me, since —"

"I know," I sneered back. "You get paid by the hour."

"That's right," he said, leaning back in his chair with his arms crossed.

Another silent stare-down between us. I lost again, breaking eye contact and looking back at my textbook. I read over the problem again, and it still didn't make sense.

"*Come on*, man," Eddie said, checking his watch again.

I was getting seriously ticked off. After all, he was supposed to be helping me.

Eddie tilted the chair back, so it was balancing on the back two legs and it creaked like it might break.

"Hey, my Mum doesn't like us to do that," I told him.

"So?"

"So cut it out."

"Make me," he said, with a laugh.

I was about to jump up and do just that when Wendy walked in from the kitchen. She barely looked at us, but as she walked behind Eddie Bosko, she shoved his chair forward.

Eddie had to catch himself so he wouldn't slam face-first into the table.

"Hey," he snapped, spinning around in his seat to confront her. "What's your —"

"It's a chair, not a ride, you moron," Wendy said, and kept walking.

Eddie Bosko watched her go, his mouth hanging open for a change.

Who's the flounder now?

I almost started laughing, but held it in.

"Who was that?" he finally asked.

"My sister." I told him. Obviously.

He didn't say anything else, but sat there with a dazed look on his face. I was willing to bet no one had ever dared to call Eddie Bosko a moron before. And lived, anyway.

"So, we're trying to figure out how long the trip takes, right?" I asked.

"Huh?" Eddie grunted.

"The problem. It's about travel time, not distance." I waited. "Isn't it?"

"I guess," he said, looking toward the stairway. "What's her name?"

"Uh," I scanned the question again. "It's just guys. Mark and Paul."

"No, your sister."

"What?"

"What's her name?"

"Wendy," I told him, as I continued to read.

If Mark was leaving Winnipeg at eight in the morning and wanted to meet Paul in Regina, how long was it going to take him to get there?

"Does she have a boyfriend?"

I glanced up at Eddie Bosko, who was still watching the stairs. "Wendy? I don't know. I think they broke up or something."

"How old is she?"

"Sixteen."

He spun around to face me. "Sixteen?"

"Yeah, you know. The one that comes after fifteen." I tried to get back on topic. "If Mark was going 70 kilometres an hour —"

"Does she go to Cutter Bay?"

What was his problem? "Last time I checked, it's the only high school here."

We got back to work, and after a few more questions, I felt like I was actually starting to get it. I liked the way he had shown me to ignore all the extra details and focus on the numbers. The more we did, the more they made sense.

Wendy came downstairs and before I knew it, Eddie Bosko was pushing what was left of the cookies toward her.

"Want some?"

Wendy looked at him, then at the cookies, most of which were broken. She rolled her eyes. "Yeah, right. Not after you losers have mauled them."

"They're really good," Eddie called after her, but she'd already disappeared into the kitchen.

I started to read out loud. "Claire and Samantha are selling Girl Guide cookies, and —"

"I'm thirsty," Eddie said, pushing his seat back and standing up.

I pointed to his glass of milk. It was still half full.

"No," he said, shaking his head and moving toward the kitchen. "I need some water or something. My throat's really dry."

This was getting suspicious.

When he came back, he had a glass of water and a red face.

"What's wrong?" I asked.

"Nothing."

"Your face is all red."

"I'm warm."

Very suspicious.

We did a couple more problems and then the doorbell rang.

When I answered it, I found a teeny lady with a pointy nose and beady eyes on the front step.

"Hello there. I'm Mrs. Bosko," she said.

The gorilla's mother looked like a baby bird?

"Uh, hi. I'm Jonathan." I opened the door wider so she could come inside.

"Are you ready?' she asked Eddie.

"I guess so," he said, packing up his bag. The whole time, he was staring at the kitchen door.

I grabbed his jacket from the closet, more than ready for him to leave. "Thanks for your help," I told him, and actually meant it. I may not have had fun hanging out with him, but I *had* made some Math progress. "I'll see you at school."

I'd never seen anyone take so long to put a jacket on. It was like he was moving in slow motion.

"I can come over again tomorrow, you know," Eddie said.

"No, you can't," Mrs. Bosko told him. "We're having dinner at Grandma's."

Eddie Bosko not only had a mother, but a grandma?

"Maybe on the weekend?" he said to me, hopefully.

"I think we have some family stuff going on," I lied. "Plus the game and everything."

Eddie Bosko frowned.

Wendy walked in, the phone stuck to her ear. She walked past us and smiled at Mrs. Bosko with the sweet and innocent look she saved for adults. Eddie waved at my sister, who barely glanced at him and definitely didn't wave back.

"I see," Mrs. Bosko said, watching Wendy climb the stairs.

And suddenly I saw too. Eddie Bosko had a weakness.

His kryptonite . . . was Wendy.

Chapter Ten

The next morning, I practically jumped out of bed the second I heard Mum coming down the hallway. "I'm up!" I called out to her, before she even had a chance to tap on my door.

"A feather could knock me over," she said, whatever that meant.

I zipped into the shower, humming to myself. All it took was one afternoon, just one stinking tutoring session, and everything had turned around for me. Math was kind of making some sense *and* Eddie Bosko was quite possibly at my mercy (well, Wendy's anyway). And in unrelated but good news, I'd known the answer to Big Danny Donlin's trivia question the night before.

Big Danny asked, "What position did Gordie Howe play?"

Easy peasy. The same position as me, which was right wing. And if he'd asked, I also could have told him that Gordie scored more than 800 goals in his career. Eight hundred and one, to be precise.

Awesome.

When I was out of the shower, I threw on my sweats and

met Mum downstairs. My bag was already packed and wait-ing by the front door. My stomach was growling for bacon, eggs and hash browns. Luckily, toast and yogurt could work too, and I smiled all the way through breakfast.

On the way to practice, Mum and I listened to the news Well, she listened to it while I daydreamed about starting for the Canucks.

He shoots, he scores!

"You're in an awfully good mood," Mum said.

"I know," I told her.

"It's nice to see you back to normal."

It was nice to feel that way, too.

In the locker room, I put on my gear while Kenny and Jason talked about a movie I'd never seen.

After a couple of minutes, Eddie Bosko walked into the room.

"Uh, hey," he said, dropping his bag next to mine. "How's it going?"

"Fine." I had him right where I wanted him!

He unzipped his bag and pulled out his shoulder pads. "So, I was thinking we could meet up again on Monday."

I glanced up and saw both Kenny and Jason staring at us.

"To study?" I asked, nice and clearly, so they wouldn't get the wrong idea. It wasn't like we were friends.

"Well, yeah. I was thinking we could go over some frac-tions and stuff."

"Monday could work," I said, with a shrug, then decid-ed to test my theory. "Why don't we meet at your place?"

Eddie Bosko shook his head. "Probably better at yours."

"Why?" I asked, casually, like it didn't matter. I had the power for once, and I was loving it!

"I just think your house is set up better for studying. My brother would get in the way."

"So would my sister," I told him.

"Do you think so?" he asked, and by the hope in his voice, I knew I had him.

Kryptonite!

I pretended to think. "Actually, I think she's got volleyball practice on Monday, so maybe we'll be okay."

Eddie Bosko licked his lips and actually looked nervous. "Now that I'm thinking about it, Tuesday might work better. That way my brother can drop me off."

"But I thought you said —"

"Definitely Tuesday," he told me.

"Sure," I said. Now I knew what Godzilla felt like, messing with all the tiny humans. Who was in charge now?

When we got out onto the ice, I was feeling stronger, faster and better than ever. I guess it was adrenaline that had me skating harder than anyone else.

"Nice work, McDonald," Coach O'Neal said.

When he put out the cones and we took turns weaving in and out of them with the puck, finishing up with a shot on goal, I scored every time. Eddie Bosko missed twice.

Ha!

I knew I shouldn't have been happy about that, but I couldn't help it.

"Man, you're on fire today," Kenny said, slapping me on the back.

"Thanks."

"Your Mum must have put an extra something in the cereal this morning."

"Yeah, like steroids," Matt said, laughing. "I can't believe you beat Bosko on the laps."

Neither could I. And things went just as well for me at school. At least until Math class, that is.

James picked up the homework assignments, and when I dug in my bag I realized I hadn't even thought about my Math homework the night before. The stuff Eddie Bosko and I had done was just random questions for practise. Mr. Holloway had assigned something totally different!

Nuts!

James stood next to my desk, waiting as I shook my head.

"You didn't do it?" he asked.

"Nope."

"You must be crazy," he said, moving to collect Danielle Borthwick's paper.

I watched as even Kenny turned in the assignment.

"Mr. McDonald," Mr. Holloway said, from the front of the class. "Will you join me at the board?"

I got up from my seat and walked toward him. Please, let it be a word problem. I know what to do. Just ignore all the extra stuff and focus on the numbers.

Kenny covered his eyes and shook his head, like he knew I was doomed, but there was a chance I wasn't. It was entirely possible that I could answer whatever question was coming my way, and the whole class would be shocked.

Mr. Holloway most of all.

Please, let it be a word problem.

I stood at the board and waited while Mr. Holloway read a question. About fractions.

Nuts!

Why did it have to be fractions?

"Could you please repeat it?" I asked, when he was done.

"That depends on whether you are simply stalling, Mr. McDonald."

"No," I told him. "I just want to make sure I got all the info."

"The what?" he asked, frowning.

"Sorry. I meant the information."

"Thank you. This is not the place for jargon, slang or abbreviations."

"I know," I sighed. It also wasn't the place for me to wow anybody. Obviously.

I thought about one of the questions I'd done with Eddie the day before. It was about the number of hot dog buns, hamburger buns, patties and dogs for a summer barbecue. Even though part of me had wanted to solve the problem the way Mum did, by cutting the extra dogs in half and putting them in the hamburger buns, I knew that wasn't a Math solution. Just like I knew the jumbled bunch of numbers Mr. Holloway had given me couldn't be figured out like a word problem.

I glanced over my shoulder at Eddie Bosko, who nodded, like he was encouraging me. Encouraging me to do what, though? What did I know about stupid fractions? I turned back to the board and tried to work my way through the question, but none of it was making sense. Even worse, whenever I started to write something on the board, Mr. Holloway would make a "tsk" noise that had me reaching for the eraser.

After three minutes that felt like three hours, he finally let me go back to my seat.

"Too bad they don't make Math steroids," Kenny whispered.

For the rest of class, I did my best to concentrate, but

my best still wasn't enough. Was Math ever going to be easy? I stared out the window and wished I was on the ice, knowing the rink was the only place things ever really went my way.

* * *

At the end of the day, Kenny and I walked home together.

"Rough day, eh?" he asked.

"Yup."

"Mr. Holloway kind of has it in for you, doesn't he?"

"It sure feels like it. He's always making me go up to the board and everything."

"How did it go with Bosko yesterday?"

"Fine," I told him. "We worked on word problems and it was really helping, but —"

"Mr. Holloway asked about fractions," Kenny said.

"Exactly. I don't know how I'm ever going to learn all this stuff."

"Me neither."

"I wish all I had to do was play hockey."

"That would be awesome!"

"I know!"

"I've been practising shots against the garage and stuff. You know, trying to get better."

"That's cool," I told him. And it was. Kenny needed all the help he could get.

"I'm excited about the game this weekend."

"Me too," I said.

"I won't be starting, but you have a good chance, don't you think?"

"I hope so." I didn't want to say anything to jinx it, but I'd been working out a plan to guarantee starting and I was pretty sure it would work.

"The way you were playing this morning, I think you're in."

"Thanks, Kenny." Between my hard work and my secret plan, I figured he was right. And I loved thinking about it.

* * *

At dinner that night, Mum brought up something I had no interest in thinking *or* talking about. But I had no choice.

"So, parent-teacher interviews are next week," she said.

Uh-oh.

"Yup," I told her.

"Pardon me?"

"Yes, they are." Sometimes it seemed like everyone cared way too much about grammar.

"Monday night. Is there anything I need to know up front?" she asked. She was probably remembering all the other times she'd gone and been disappointed by what my teachers had to say.

"I don't think so," I told her.

"Any teachers you particularly want me to see?"

"Uh, not that I can think of." But I could think of one she should avoid. Maybe Mr. Holloway would catch laryngitis over the weekend and have to stay home. Maybe he'd get stuck in an elevator. For a week.

Anything was possible, right?

If Mr. Holloway wasn't there, Mum could just talk to my English teacher, which would be good, and Socials with Mr. Marshall would be okay, too. If she finished off with a chat about my P.E. class, the whole thing could actually be totally fine. And with that, I found myself hoping that for once in my life, parent-teacher interviews might be a breeze.

But what I should have prepared for was a hurricane.

Chapter Eleven

By the time game day rolled around on Saturday, I'd missed one of Big Danny Donlin's questions.

When he asked which NHL team the first woman had played for, I figured it was a trick question.

Come on. Girls in the NHL?

But it turned out that a woman called Manon Rhéaume had tended goal in a couple of exhibition games for the Tampa Bay Lightning, and won a silver medal for women's hockey at the Olympics.

I had to admit, that was pretty cool. Awesome, actually.

I was learning a lot from my studying, like what city the very first NHL game was played in. My first guess was Toronto, but then I thought it might be Ottawa. It turned out to be Montreal.

I also read about some stuff I already knew, like who was considered the best defenseman ever.

Bobby Orr. No doubt about it.

And if Big Danny Donlin ever asked which team had won the most Stanley Cups?

I knew it was the Canadiens.

I could hardly wait until the last day of the contest, when it would be my turn to call in and claim the big prize. My first live Canucks game. My shot from centre ice.

I was getting closer to the dream every day.

* * *

"Ready?" Dad asked, poking his head into my room, where I'd just finished packing my gear for the game.

"Definitely," I said, smiling. "I think we're going to win this one." My secret plan was going into effect that very morning. That meant Eddie Bosko was going down in flames while I was the star of the game. I couldn't wait.

"I hope so," he said, carrying the bag for me.

"What if we go undefeated this year?" I asked, following him down the stairs and into the dining room.

Mum had made French toast, which wasn't a favourite of mine, but still made the top twenty.

"Isn't this your first game?" Wendy asked, rolling her eyes. She was reading some goofy romance book and eating half a grapefruit. Gross, on both counts.

"So?" I asked.

"Don't get ahead of yourself, Nugget." She stuck her nose back in her book.

I stared at her for a second, knowing something was wrong, but not quite sure what it was. And then it hit me. She was still in her pyjamas!

"You aren't coming to watch?" I asked. Wendy was supposed to show up and throw Eddie's game off! She was supposed to smile and wink, or whatever it was girls did, so the gorilla would turn into a monkey on the ice. I was counting on it.

"Come on, Wendy," Dad called out from the kitchen.

"Family time," Mum said, reaching down to squeeze my sister's shoulders.

"But I'm reading," she whined.

"I'm pretty sure you can read at the rink," Mum said.

"Yeah, right." My laugh sounded panicked, which I was. I needed her to be there! "You won't be able to keep your eyes off the game."

"Give me a break," Wendy said, laughing.

"I'm serious," I told her, trying to build the excitement. "McDonald fakes left, then right! He's going for it, fans! He's lining up the puck for a wicked slapshot. Here it comes, here it comes. He shoots, he scores!"

"We'll see about that," she said. "Give me a couple of minutes to get dressed, okay?"

Yes! Eddie Bosko was toast! I counted my lucky stars that the plan was still a go and as we waited for Wendy out in the van, I remembered the flounder look on Bosko's face when he met my sister.

It was going to be so cool to watch him go down the tubes.

On the drive to the rink, I sat in the back with Wendy, who told me the whole plot of the book she was reading, like I cared. I pretended to be interested, knowing she was my golden ticket to greatness. My plan was perfect.

Or so I thought.

* * *

When I got to the locker room, most of the guys were already dressed and hanging around, talking. I pulled on my gear and sat next to Kenny on one of the benches.

"I wonder who Coach decided to start," he said, quietly, tilting his head at Eddie Bosko and raising his eyebrows at me.

"I don't know," I told him, thinking about all the effort

I'd put in at our practices. It should be me. Then again, if Eddie started, that just meant his downfall would happen early in the game. And that was okay with me, too.

Eddie Bosko glanced over and gave me a quick nod, so I nodded back, but didn't say anything. I felt a tiny bit guilty. He'd actually helped me with Math and I'd returned the favour by plotting his destruction on the ice. But, as he loved to remind me, he was getting *paid* to help me, and that didn't make us friends.

"Okay, guys, are we ready?" Coach O'Neal asked, clapping his hands to get our attention.

"Yes," a few of us said.

Coach's eyes moved over each of us, slowly. "What is this, a kindergarten class?" He shook his head. "Let's try that again. Are you ready?"

"Yes!" we shouted, raising our sticks in the air like we were going into battle, which we were.

"That's better. You guys had me scared for a second, there." He checked his clipboard. "Okay, I want McDaniel, Bechter, Simpson, Chen and McDonald up first."

I smiled. I was starting, which meant my hard work had paid off! I glanced at Eddie Bosko, who was concentrating on taping his stick. Or pretending to, anyway.

That guilty feeling nudged me again. There was a part of me that actually felt sorry for him. After all, he had a new uniform, new teammates and the brand new experience of starting on the bench.

I shook it off. The other part of me was too excited to worry about anyone else. The season was starting, and it was going to be the best one ever!

I thumped Kenny on the back as we left the locker room and headed out to the ice.

"Awesome," he said, elbowing me back. "Starting right wing. You did it."

"So will you," I told him. "Guaranteed he'll play you first period."

"I hope so," Kenny said. "My granny's here."

I remembered her from a couple of games last season. She looked like a granny, but she acted like a fan. She even yelled at the ref and made me kind of glad my own granny lived in Burnaby.

We had a few minutes before the game started, so me and the rest of the guys warmed up on the ice. I skated some laps, checking out the Bayview Turtles at the same time. The opposing team was about as intimidating as their name. Most of the guys were average size, except for a couple of smaller ones.

Small, but bigger than me, of course.

"I thought the Tykes played on Sundays," one of them called out to me as I skated past.

I ignored him.

"What is he, a second grader?"

Very funny.

"He's probably somebody's kid brother," another guy said.

"Yeah, like a mascot."

I'd heard it all before, year after year.

Wait until they saw my slapshot, though. That would stop them cold. And when my stupid growth spurt finally happened, I'd never have to listen to the "short" stuff again.

"Who is *that*?" one of the Turtles asked.

"Geez! Hercules, maybe?"

I didn't have to turn around to know who they were talking about. I'd thought practically the same thing when I first saw our giant.

"Oh, man. That's Eddie Bosko," one of the guys groaned.

"I thought we didn't have to play him for a couple of weeks."

"Looks like the Cougars brought in a ringer," one of the guys sighed.

I skated away, already tired of hearing it. *I* was the one they should have been worried about, the one who was going to skate circles around them.

I took some practice shots and was happy when every single one went in.

The buzzer sounded and it was game time!

We got into position and I found myself face to face with Sean Sanders. He glanced at me, and I growled back.

I could tell from his expression that he remembered me from last season. I'd shoulder-checked him more than once. He let out a slow breath and I smiled to myself.

I was small, but he was scared.

Mum would say that shouldn't have made me feel good, but it did. Even though he wasn't looking at me anymore, I stared him down for a few more seconds, until the ref dropped the puck.

Game on!

Jeremy took possession and passed to Colin, who took off toward the net. The kid covering me was left at centre ice and he probably didn't even know I was gone until I was halfway to the net. All I heard was a cheering crowd, the scrape of blades against the ice and my own breathing.

Come on, Colin!

I felt more alive than I did anywhere else.

Colin looked like he was going for the shot, so I lined myself up in case the goalie deflected it. I crouched, ready to spring into action if the puck came anywhere near me.

107

And it did!

Colin's shot bounced off the post and raced toward me. I clipped it with my stick, so it would drop back to the ice, then skated toward the goal. I first faked a shot, then zipped around the back of the net. I knew the goalie would have a hard time seeing me behind him, so I took my time, playing with the puck while the crowd shouted for me to shoot. One of the Turtles made some choppy moves toward me with his stick, but I made a tight turn around the left side of the net.

The goalie was still looking right!

Perfect!

In one quick move, I whipped the puck into the corner of the net.

Yes!

The first goal of the season was mine!

All of the Cougars skated up to me, cheering and punching me in the arm.

"Nice one, Nugget!"

"Way to go, man!"

I was super excited and proud of myself, but I didn't let on that it was a big deal. I just skated back toward the centre line, prepared to either protect our goal or steal the puck.

Or both.

Four minutes into the game, Colin scored with a beautiful shot that went right through the goalie's legs. Just after the six minute mark, the Turtles managed to get one in, and then I scored again!

At seven minutes, Coach O'Neal called a time out.

And that's when it all fell apart.

Chapter Twelve

When the ref blew the whistle, we skated over to the team box and leaned against the railing. I was a little out of breath, but I could tell how much my summer conditioning had paid off. After all, Colin and Patrick were both panting.

"Good playing out there, guys." Coach said. "Good hustle, nice teamwork. I like what I'm seeing."

It was exactly what I wanted to hear, what we all wanted to hear. The five of us made an awesome starting lineup, and I was relieved Coach could see that right off the bat. And if I continued to prove myself (which was exactly what I planned to do), there would be no stopping me. Short or not, I'd finally be able to convince Coach to let me play against the Shoreline Sharks. Those monsters wouldn't know what hit them, and even better than was the fact that it was going to be my best season ever.

And Eddie Bosko was stuck on the bench.

If he'd looked my way, I would have smiled or something, but his eyes were glued to Coach. For a second I wondered if Eddie's family was up in the stands, wondering why he wasn't on the ice. I pushed the thought away, because I had other things to think about.

Like playing.

The most I'd ever scored in a single game was three goals, but what if I scored four? Five? Or more? I was about to become a statistic worthy of *Shoot! Third Edition*, as soon as —

"I'm going to mix things up a bit," Coach said.

Mix things up?

"McCafferty, you take over for Chen."

Too bad, since Patrick had been making some sweet passes. But David "Bedhead" McCafferty was a pretty good replacement. He could feed me the puck and when he did —

Coach interrupted my thought. "Bosko, I want you in for McDonald."

"What?" I practically croaked. He was taking me out? I just *scored*! Twice!

It didn't make sense.

Eddie Bosko stood up and grabbed his stick. He walked toward the ice and there was only one thing I could do. It might not have been fair, but I needed to get back on the ice as soon as possible, and that meant one thing. It was time for the kryptonite.

As I passed Eddie Bosko on my way back into the box, I looked up into the stands and shook my head. "Oh man," I groaned, "I hate it when my sister comes to the games."

Eddie spun around to see where I was looking. "She's here?"

"Yup," I said, rolling my eyes. "Just great."

When he looked for her, I watched his face for signs of the flounder.

110

I saw nothing, so I gave it another shot. "Wendy McDonald, our number one fan," I sighed.

"Cool." Eddie Bosko smiled and stepped onto the ice.

What? *Cool?* He was supposed to get all weird and nervous, like he did during our study session. He was supposed to flop around on the ice like he'd never worn skates before. He was supposed to screw up, not *smile*.

I frowned and sunk down on the bench, disappointed. Usually I saved my miscalculations for Math class.

Kryptonite?

Yeah, right.

Eddie Bosko was *happy* my stupid sister was watching him play.

The ref blew the whistle, Eddie Bosko raced toward the puck like his life depended on it, and I was the one left with the flounder face. He shoulder-checked the Turtles centre and stole the puck in less than two seconds, then maneuvered around two other players to take a shot on goal. He scored.

Nuts!

The crowd leapt to their feet, cheering, and my stomach sunk toward my skates.

Eddie Bosko glanced up in the stands to where my family was sitting, smiled, then re-focused on the game.

What had I done? Wendy was supposed to ruin his game, not *improve* it!

For the next six minutes, I watched Eddie Bosko steal, pass and shoot until the score was Cutter Bay Cougars, 8, Turtles, 2.

The worst part was that I didn't even care that we were winning. After all, Eddie Bosko was playing me right out of the starting lineup. My whole stinking plan had backfired, big time.

Coach didn't put me in again until second period, and when he did, I played harder than ever before. I had to undo the damage! I fought for the puck and managed to score another goal.

Take that!

I assisted David for another point, but I knew it wasn't enough and I started to panic. Suddenly, I couldn't get my head or anything else into the game.

That's when the ref called me for high-sticking.

High-sticking!

I had to spend two precious minutes in the penalty box. *Come on!*

With only four of us on the ice, the Turtles were taking advantage of a power play while I was practically drooling to get back in the game.

When they finally scored on us and my penalty ended, I shot out of the box like a tornado. Right away, I skated behind a Turtle and tried to swerve around him to steal the puck, but I accidentally tripped him with my stick instead.

Back in the box for another two minutes!

I couldn't believe it! I *never* got penalties. Dad had always taught me to play by the rules, and somehow I was blowing it!

The Turtles didn't score, so I had to spend the whole stinking penalty sitting in the box with a red face, knowing I was going to get an earful from Dad on the way home. And I was pretty sure Coach would have some choice words for me too.

Eddie came out for a breather, but sat at the other end of the team bench, focused on the game.

Kenny was sitting closest to me, but whenever he tried

to talk over the wall of the penalty box, I stopped him. I didn't need someone to make me feel better. I needed to get back onto the ice.

When my second penalty was just about over, I was on my feet, ready to get out there and rock the rink.

"Sit down," Coach O'Neal said.

"What?" I asked, totally confused.

"I'm putting Bosko back in."

"But —"

"You need to get some control over your stick, Nugget."

I couldn't believe it!

"I was just —"

"We can't keep handing them power plays."

I didn't even look into the stands, because I knew that all I'd see were the disappointed expressions on Mum and Dad's faces. I didn't think I could feel any worse, but when third period rolled around and Coach left Eddie Bosko in, I knew I was done for the day. Aside from the Shoreline games, I'd never spent two full periods on the bench!

"Man, you've got to watch the penalties, Nugget," Kenny said.

I was so ticked off, I didn't even think before asking him, "What do you know about it? You're a benchwarmer, Kenny."

My best friend on the team stared at me for a second, and I felt my stomach drop even lower.

"You've spent more time on the bench than me today," he said quietly.

I felt like a total jerk.

He turned away from me to watch Eddie Bosko score yet another goal.

"He's awesome," Jeremy said.

"Best right winger we've got," Kenny added, nodding slowly.

Ouch!

Eddie Bosko skated backward to centre ice, like a big showboat. Was he waiting for people to throw him flowers or something?

It was hockey, for Pete's sake, not figure skating.

* * *

We won the game, 14 to 6.

It was our highest score ever and the guys were thrilled. Everyone but me, anyway. I was the last to head for the locker room. I didn't want to listen to everyone congratulate Bosko on his awesome game, so I walked really slowly.

How had my master plan turned into such a disaster?

"Have we got a problem, McDonald?" Coach asked, from behind me.

Oh, brother. "No."

"Something you want to talk about?"

"No," I sighed.

"An issue with Bosko?"

"Yes!" I said, turning to face him. "He's stealing my position and —"

"No one is stealing anything."

"He is. I was just —"

"Nugget, you're giving it away."

What?"

"No I'm not. I was playing —"

"Sloppy," Coach finished for me.

I started to argue, but knew he was right.

"Two penalties in what, four minutes? That's not like you."

"I know." I frowned.

"You're a much better player than that." Coach scratched his forehead. "Do you understand why I kept you out of the game?"

"Yeah."

"We can't afford to play four against five because of stupid mistakes."

"I know."

"This isn't Atom anymore. Sure, I need guys who play hard, but they also need to play by the rules."

"The tripping was an accident," I told him. It was true.

"But the high-sticking wasn't," Coach said, quietly.

Also true. "Sorry, Coach," I said, feeling my face turn red again.

"So," he said, patting me on the back, "lesson learned?"

"Yeah."

"Good, because we need you when we play the Thunderbirds next week."

There was something I desperately wanted to ask him, but I was scared of the answer. I took a deep breath and asked anyway.

"Am I starting?"

He looked at me for a moment. "We'll see how things go at practice."

"Oh." I couldn't hide my disappointment.

He frowned. "That isn't a 'no,' Nugget."

"I know."

"It just means you have to show me what we both know you're capable of."

"Okay," I said, nodding as I opened the locker room door.

As soon as I did, I could hear the excited voices of my teammates. I walked down the hallway, thinking about what

Coach had said. It was all about proving myself, and I could do that. I hadn't been playing hockey for my whole life just so I could ride the bench. I wanted to start.

And if I did my best, there was no reason I couldn't.

Right?

Chapter Thirteen

"So, that was quite the game," Dad said, glancing at me in the rear-view mirror on the drive home.

"Yes, it was," I agreed, quietly. I didn't want to talk about it.

"You were a goon out there," Wendy said, shaking her head. "A total goon."

"I was trying to win," I muttered.

"You should have been trying to play well, Jonathan," Dad said.

"I *was*."

"We were there, honey," Mum said. "You were reckless."

"They were minor penalties," I reminded all of them. You'd think I'd tried to run someone over with the Zamboni!

"You'd better be a little more careful at the next game," Dad said. "Winning is great, but so is fair play."

"Do we have to keep talking about this?" I asked.

"Not if we've come to an understanding," Mum said.

"We have," I told her, then stared out the window.

* * *

I spent the rest of the day cleaning my room. Mum said I had to, or else, and I didn't even want to know what that meant.

After dinner, I tuned in to Big Danny Donlin's show at just the right moment.

"Tomorrow is the big night, folks," he said.

"What big night?" Dad asked, coming into the kitchen for some milk.

"The grand prize. They're giving away the shot from centre ice tomorrow," I whispered.

"Wow," he said, leaning against the counter to listen.

"Tonight's question, for a stick signed by none other than Sergei Federov —"

"Holy smokes," I whispered. Now that was a prize!

"Do you want to go for it?" Dad asked.

I shook my head. "You're only allowed to win once."

"What if you know the answer today, but not tomorrow?"

That would stink, one hundred percent, but it was the risk I had to take. "I want the shot more than anything, Dad. I have to go for it."

"Are you ready?" Big Danny Donlin asked his listeners.

"Yes," Dad and I said, smiling at each other.

"We're looking for caller number seven to tell us which team Mark Messier scored the most goals for?"

"The Rangers!" I shouted.

For a Sergei Federov stick? Was Big Danny Donlin *crazy*? It was way too easy!

"I think it was the Oilers," Dad said.

What? "But Gretzky —"

Dad looked down at the floor while he thought it out. "Gretzky may have scored more goals than Messier for the

Oilers, but they're asking where *Messier* scored the most. He played for three or four teams during his career, and . . ." Dad scratched his head. "It can't be the Canucks."

"No way," I agreed.

"Who's on the line?" Big Danny Donlin asked.

"Paul, from Kitchener."

"Ontario?" Big Danny sounded shocked.

"Yeah, I'm visiting my sister."

"Okay, then. You're caller number seven, Paul. What's your answer?"

"The Oilers?"

"That sounded more like a question."

"Sorry. The Oilers."

"You are correct!"

I had to admit, Dad really knew his stuff. "You'll help me tomorrow night, right, Dad?"

"Of course," he said. "No guarantees of a win, though. I'm betting the final question will be tough."

He was probably right.

* * *

The next night, I grabbed plates so I could get the table ready for dinner. It was my turn to set and Dad's turn to cook sloppy joes, which I loved.

"I think we're missing some food groups, here," Mum said, eyeing the pot of bubbling goodness and pulling some vegetables from the fridge. "Can you put together a salad, Wend?"

My sister got to work, slicing and dicing celery, tomatoes and cucumbers.

"So, tonight's the big night, eh, Jonathan?" Dad asked, sprinkling some salt and pepper into the pot.

"What big night?" Mum asked.

"The final question from Big Danny Donlin."

"Are we supposed to know what you're talking about?" Wendy asked.

"It's a radio show with a trivia question every night —"

"Like history and stuff?" Wendy asked.

"No, hockey."

"Oh, brother," she said, rolling her eyes.

"What do you win?" Mum asked.

"They've had some good prizes every night, but tonight they're giving away tickets to a Canucks game and —"

"In Vancouver?" Wendy asked.

"Duh. That's where they play," I told her.

"He gets to go to Vancouver?" Wendy gasped at Mum.

"He hasn't won anything," Mum told her.

"Thanks for the vote of confidence," I muttered.

"I meant *yet*, honey." She winked at me. "So, a Canucks game would be exciting."

"Exciting? It would only be the most awesome thing I've ever seen," I told her. "And that isn't even the best part." I took a deep breath, since the idea of it had me practically hyperventilating. "During the game, the winner gets to take a shot from centre ice and —"

"With a goalie?" Wendy asked.

"Empty net," I said, without looking at her. "And when I score, I get signed stuff and $5,000!"

"Let's not get ahead of ourselves, little brother," Wendy said.

"What?"

"You haven't even heard the question yet, so you don't know if you'll have the answer, and even if you do, you've got to be the phone call that gets through."

"I will be," I told her. "Caller number seven. It's my destiny."

"Destiny?" Dad asked, raising his eyebrow at me, then Mum.

"Destiny," I said again.

"Well, until the big moment, you're destined to finish setting the table," Mum said, pointing toward the dining room.

"I'm on top of it," I told her, grabbing extra napkins for our sloppy joes.

* * *

All the way through dinner, while Wendy was talking about some new hair place she wanted to try, I was repeating Big Danny Donlin's phone number in my head, over and over again. I couldn't believe the grand prize day had finally arrived. I was nervous and excited, but mostly excited. My emotions didn't affect my appetite though, and I ended up going back for seconds.

I glanced at the clock in the kitchen.

One hour and twenty minutes, and counting.

While Mum and Dad told Wendy that her taste in expensive salons might mean she should start thinking about a part time job, I tried to think of the MVP for every Stanley Cup, beginning with last year and going backwards.

I thought it would be easy, and it should have been.

One hour and eleven minutes.

I cleared the table and loaded the dishwasher to kill some time, and it wasn't even my turn.

Back in my room, I flipped through *Shoot! Third Edition*, but whenever I came across a fact I didn't know, it totally freaked me out. I should have spent more time studying!

Forty minutes to go.

I slowly turned the pages, trying to memorize them. What if the information I needed wasn't even in *Shoot!*

Third Edition? What if it was in the *fourth* edition, which was *still* on backorder at Chapters? I'd seen the cover, but nothing else. How much information had they added?

Twenty-three minutes.

My palms were sweating.

The Hockey Hall of Fame is located in Toronto.

Alexei Kovalev was the first Russian player to be drafted in the first round for the NHL.

The Detroit Red Wings were the first team to put numbers on their jersey sleeves.

Sergei Federov wore number eighteen when he played in Russia.

How would I ever remember it all?

I glanced at the clock.

Six minutes.

It was almost time!

I ran downstairs and climbed up on a kitchen chair to grab the radio, so I could put it on the table.

"What are you doing?" Wendy asked, just as I lifted it, totally surprising me.

I lost my grip and tried to grab at the radio, but it slipped out of my hands.

"No!" I screamed, as I watched it fall to the ground, like slow motion, and explode into about twenty-six thousand pieces.

"What's your problem?" Wendy asked, just as Mum and Dad ran into the room.

"What happened?" Mum asked.

"Let's just say Nugget lacks a kung-fu grip," Wendy said, smirking.

"It's not funny!" I shrieked. "The contest is in, like four minutes!"

"Relax, Jonathan," Mum said. "Let's get this cleaned up."

"There's no time right now," I gasped, running toward the stairs. "I'll clean it up after the big question."

"The big question," I heard Mum ask, "is how he's going to pay for a new radio."

With my $5,000 grand prize, of course.

I raced into Mum and Dad's room and turned on Dad's alarm clock radio. He had it set to stupid CBC! I turned the dial as fast as I could to Big Danny Donlin's station and caught him going to a commercial break.

Whew!

I ran to my room to grab *Shoot! Third Edition* and raced back to Mum and Dad's, where I jumped onto the bed, messing up the quilt.

I had everything I needed. I gulped. Except a phone!

No!

I jumped off the bed again and ran downstairs. In the kitchen, Mum was already cleaning up the smashed radio.

"I promise I'll do that as soon as the contest is over," I told her, reaching for the phone.

It wasn't there.

Just an empty charger!

That was when I heard Wendy's voice in the living room and I knew she'd taken it. Getting her off the phone was always a challenge, but I was ready to tackle her, if I had to.

I ran into the living room, with my hand out, ready for her to pass it, like a baton in a relay race. Instead, she covered the mouthpiece and scowled at me. "What?"

"The contest! I need the phone."

"I'm in the middle of —"

I snatched the phone from her hand before she could

finish. "She'll call you back," I told whoever it was and hung up on them.

"What do you think you're doing?" Wendy shouted, chasing after me.

"Getting my chance at centre ice!" I called over my shoulder as I ran up the stairs at top speed.

I leaped onto Mum and Dad's bed just as Big Danny Donlin came back on the air. "Let's get this grand prize rolling," he said.

Yes!

My hands were shaking and sweaty but I dialed the number I'd memorized. Well, all but the very last digit. As soon as I heard the question, I'd hit number four, and hopefully I'd be caller number seven. I'd been planning my strategy from the very beginning and if I was caller three or something, I was ready to hang up and hit "redial" right away.

I crossed my legs, then straightened them, then tugged at the neck of my sweatshirt.

Why was it so hot upstairs?

Penguins. Bruins. Flames. Leafs. Ducks.

I took a deep breath.

Hull. Lemieux. Brodeur. Orr. Roy.

The dial tone started to beep from waiting so long.

Nuts!

I hung up and dialed again, all but that last number, then turned to get more comfortable on the bed. I was surprised to see my whole family was in the doorway, watching me.

"This will only take a minute," I whispered.

Mum nodded, leaning against Dad.

Wendy was silent, but I could tell she'd have a lot to say later.

"And tonight's big question is all about goaltending," Big Danny Donlin said.

"Do you know anything about goaltending?" Wendy asked.

"Shh," I told her, as my brain practically exploded with facts.

The Canucks goalie is also their team captain.

A puck is made of vulcanized rubber.

Terry Sawchuk had the most career shutouts.

A goal judge, not the ref, decides when a goal is scored.

And, of course, scoring three goals in a single game is called a hat trick.

"Here we go," Big Danny Donlin continued. "For two tickets to a Canucks game and the chance to score from centre ice and win $5,000 —"

"Five thousand dollars?" Mum gasped.

"I already told you that." I smiled, picturing a wallet so fat it wouldn't fit in my pocket.

"When's the game?" Wendy asked.

Me, Mum and Dad all said "Shh!" at the same time.

"We're looking for caller number seven to tell us which goalie had stitches painted on his mask every time he was hit in the face."

I let out a shaky breath.

"Good grief," Dad sighed. "Sorry, kiddo."

I wasn't sorry at all. I was stunned. "I know it," I whispered, hitting 4 as fast as I could.

"What?" Dad gasped.

"I know it," I said, louder.

"No way," Wendy said.

The phone was ringing.

"How on earth do you know it?" Mum asked.

It rang again and I could barely breathe.

A third ring.

"This is Big —" a voice said in my ear, then the radio screeched.

"Turn it off," Dad said, reaching past me to unplug the clock radio. "It's interfering."

"Yowzers!" Big Danny Donlin said. "I'm definitely awake now. Who do I have on the line?"

"Nugget . . . I mean, Jonathan."

"And where are you from, Jonathan?"

"Cutter Bay."

"Is he on?" Wendy whispered.

"Shh," Mum told her again.

"And you have an answer for me?" Big Danny Donlin asked.

"Yes."

"So, caller number seven, which goaltender wore a mask covered with stitches?"

I cleared my throat. "Gerry Cheevers."

"Jonathan from Cutter Bay, you are one hundred per-cent correct!"

I couldn't believe it. "I won?" I gasped.

My whole family started jumping up and down, waving their arms in the air.

"You won, and I'm going to put you on hold so one of the guys can fill you in on the details."

There was only one detail I cared about, and that was scoring from centre ice.

Chapter Fourteen

It turned out that the Canucks game was a month away and I'd have to wait four whole weeks before I had my chance at the shot.

Unfortunately, waiting for the Canucks to play wasn't the only thing I had to worry about. In all of the contest excitement, I'd totally forgotten about parent-teacher interviews.

But Mum and Dad hadn't.

I was busy reading the last chapter of *Over the Moon* on Monday night when they got back from the school.

"Jonathan, will you come down here, please?" Dad called from downstairs.

"Just a second," I called back, trying to read faster. I couldn't believe how much I cared how the book was going to end.

"Now!" Mum shouted.

Uh-oh.

I slipped a bookmark between the pages and took a deep breath. What now?

When I got downstairs, Mum and Dad were sitting at the dining room table, both on the same side. There was one chair facing the two of them and when Dad tilted his head at it, I sat down.

"So, Mum said, putting both of her hands face down on the table and staring at them for a minute. "What can you tell me about Mr. Holloway's class?"

Double uh-oh.

"It's on the second floor, two doors down from the library and —"

"Not the location, Jonathan," Mum said. "The class itself."

"Um . . . I think there are maybe twenty-five kids, and of course Mr. —"

"Jonathan," Dad warned. "You know perfectly well what we're talking about."

Unfortunately, I did.

"We learned quite a bit tonight," Mum said, frowning. "Mr. Holloway went into great detail about the teacher-student relationship."

"In particular," Dad continued, "how *he* is a teacher who assigns homework and *you* are a student who doesn't complete it."

Nuts!

Who came up with the stupid idea for parent-teacher interviews, anyway? Like I needed all the grown-ups to get together and talk about me!

"I've completed some of it," I argued.

"Forty-six percent of it," Mum said.

Nuts.

Count on Mr. Holloway to give them an exact percentage.

"Look, I've been trying to —"

"Win hockey games?" Mum finished for me. "Enter trivia contests?"

My stomach twisted.

"Look, son," Dad said, leaning toward me. "As we all know, from many conversations in the past, when school suffers —"

"Hockey goes out the window," Wendy said, coming in from the kitchen. She was talking through a mouthful of mushy banana.

Yeah, yeah, yeah. I'd heard it all before. Hockey goes out the window. Blah, blah, blah. They were kidding, weren't they? I looked from one face to the other and back again, my stomach twisting tighter.

They had to be kidding!

Didn't they?

"This is no joke," Mum said. "Until you bring your Math grades up, you are officially benched."

"But —"

"This means adding an extra tutoring session every week," Mum added.

"Eddie Bosko is about to become a permanent fixture around here," Dad said. "Maybe we should prepare the guest room."

"But —"

"We're past the point of buts," Dad said, resting a hand on my shoulder and shaking his head.

"You are a very lucky boy, Jonathan McDonald," Mum said.

"I am?" I asked. It sure didn't feel like it.

"I wanted your trip to the Canucks game to be dependent on your Math grade."

I almost choked. "But I *won* the trip, and —"

"Don't worry. Your father talked me out of it," Mum interrupted. "Like I said, you're a lucky boy."

I didn't dare argue with that.

* * *

As it turned out, my parents' long talk with Mr. Holloway proved that all three grown-ups were on the exact same page, in the worst book *ever*.

I was on my way out of yet another confusing Math class on Tuesday when Mr. Holloway called me up to his desk. The last couple of kids out the door snickered, then the room was dead silent.

"Mr. McDonald," Mr. Holloway said, leaning back in his chair and looking at me over the top of his glasses.

"Yes?"

"We have been struggling this year, haven't we?"

I knew he didn't really mean "we," but me.

"Yes." I nodded.

"Homework assignments have been completed at a rather dismal rate."

I figured dismal meant bad, so I nodded again.

"Since you are a student who refuses to do the assigned work at home, I'm afraid you'll be doing it in the class-room."

Nuts!

"Do you mean standing at the board?" I asked, already dreading it.

"No."

Whew!

"Every Friday for the next three weeks, you will report to this room, immediately following the dismissal bell." He stared at me. "I will prepare a test for each week, and you must average seventy-five percent on the three tests."

Seventy-five percent!

Or what? I wanted to ask.

He must have seen the question in my eyes, because he answered it. "Or you fail this class and hockey season is over for good, Mr. McDonald."

* * *

I found Kenny in the lunchroom and sat next to him. I wanted to tell him about my serious Math problem, but I also wanted to apologise for being a jerk at Saturday's game. The rotten part was, I didn't know what to say.

"Want my oatmeal cookies?" I asked.

Kenny didn't answer. In fact, he didn't even look at me.

"Kenny," I said, nudging him with my elbow.

"Are you talking to me?" he asked.

"Yeah."

"Wow, I feel honoured." He still wouldn't look at me. Instead, he bit into a gross looking (and smelling) tuna sandwich.

I tried again. "Look, I didn't mean to —"

"Be a jerk?" he asked.

"Well . . . yeah."

"Because you were, you know." He frowned. "A total jerk."

"I know, Kenny, and I'm sorry."

"Why do you have to be so greedy about hockey?"

"I'm not, I —"

"Yes you are. Why can't you just be happy when other people score, or have an awesome game?"

"I am, it's just that —"

"You're a jerk?" he asked.

Ouch. I nodded slowly, knowing he was right. I'd been a total jerk to a kid who'd been a really good buddy, and that stunk. "Sometimes. I'm seriously sorry, Kenny."

He finally looked at me and was quiet for a few seconds. "I believe you."

"So are we okay?" I asked.

"The cookies will make it even," he said, smiling.

I handed them over and got to work on my ham and cheese sandwich.

"So, what did Mr. Holloway want?" Kenny asked, in between bites.

I explained the situation to him and watched his eyes bug out. "So, I'm stuck with a test every week, even more tutoring with Bosko and no hockey."

"You have the worst luck of any kid I know, Nugget."

I imagined what the grown-ups would think about that. I was pretty sure Mum, Dad, Coach and Mr. Holloway would all say the same thing, so I said it to Kenny. "It's not bad luck, it's bad decisions." It was true.

I took another bite of my sandwich, just as Eddie Bosko showed up at our table.

"I hear we're doing twice a week now," he said.

"Yeah."

He shrugged. "The extra work won't hurt you or my wallet."

"Great." Did he have to keep reminding me about getting paid?

"Is your sister going to be there?"

I sighed. "I have no idea. But listen, Eddie, this is serious. I need to score a seventy-five percent average on three tests."

He shrugged again. "You can probably do that."

"I can't play hockey until I do."

Eddie Bosko froze. "What are you talking about?" he asked.

"Exactly what it sounds like," I told him. "If I don't get my grades up, I don't play."

His eyebrows squished together to make an expression I'd never seen on his face before. Eddie Bosko actually looked *worried*. "But I'm not going to be here for the next game," he said.

"You're not?"

"No! And I was thinking that's okay because we cover each other so well."

"What?"

"I figured you'd play more while I'm gone and we'd still stand a chance of winning." He scowled. "If we both can't play, we're doomed."

I stared at him, trying to understand what I'd heard. "Did you just say we cover each other well?"

"Yeah. You're the best guy I've shared the position with."

"Shared?" What was he talking about? I thought we'd been fighting for it.

"Duh, Nugget." He shook his head. "I need a good partner, and you're it."

"Partner?"

Eddie Bosko turned to Kenny and asked, "Is something wrong with him?"

"It's more than one thing," Kenny told him. "In fact, I can't even count them all."

"So," I said, "this whole time we've been playing together, you wanted me to be good?"

Eddie rolled his eyes. "We're a team, man."

And that's when it hit me. Worrying about who was going to start had been a total waste of time! Neither of us could play the whole game without a break, so we needed to share the position. And even more important? If we both played well, we were a double threat to the opposing team. I never should have wanted Eddie to be a monkey on the ice, because we were supposed to be working together.

Oh brother, was I ever stupid!

"We're gonna lose this weekend," Eddie groaned. "I know it."

"Can't you change your plans?" I asked.

"No."

"Why not?" Kenny asked, sprouts trailing from his mouth like worms. How gross could one stinking sandwich get?

Eddie frowned again. "I have somewhere I need to be, okay?"

"Where?" I asked, wondering what on earth could be more important than the game.

Eddie Bosko let out a sigh. "Meeting of the Math Minds."

"What?" Kenny and I both asked.

"It's a Math competition, for the whole province."

I couldn't believe what I was hearing. "You're willing to let the Cougars lose so you can be part of a nerd herd?"

Kenny laughed and milk came out of his nose.

Yuck.

"What did you just say?" Eddie asked, leaning in close.

I cleared my throat. "Nothing, it's just —"

"Hey, I have a good reason for not being able to play. I'm not the one who can't make it because they goofed off in Math class. That's you, Nugget. You blew that on your own."

He was right, and I didn't have a comeback.

"I'll see you at your place after school," he told me. "We'll get you your seventy-five percent, but you'd better be ready to work for it."

* * *

Eddie Bosko wasn't kidding.

When he came over, it was straight to the books, with only a quick break to wolf down a bunch of Mum's brownies.

He only pulled a flounder once, and that was the first time Wendy came through the dining room to grab a snack from the kitchen.

"Hey, do you like horror movies?" he asked.

Wendy turned to face him. "You'll be living one if my brother doesn't pass Math. Get to work."

Ouch!

Eddie Bosko's face turned bright red, and from that moment on, he was more focused than ever.

Which meant I had to be too.

Chapter Fifteen

On Friday, I reported to Mr. Holloway's class and found out I had thirty minutes to complete my first test. I slowly worked my way through fifteen questions. Most of them involved calculating percentages and multiplying fractions and, thanks to Eddie Bosko, almost all of them made sense.

To my surprise, I finished a few minutes early and I stood up to turn the paper in.

"Review, Mr. McDonald," Mr. Holloway said when I was halfway up the aisle.

"But —"

"Review," he said, more firmly.

I plunked down in the closest seat to check my answers. After just a few seconds I very quietly erased and corrected one of them. Maybe he was right.

When my thirty minutes were officially up, Mr. Holloway collected my test and made me sit at my desk to wait while he marked it.

I did my best to just breathe, and when I heard him make a "tsk" noise, I closed my eyes for a few seconds and pretended I was out on the ice. I imagined that time was about to run out in a tied game and Kenny passed the puck to me.

I slipped past a defender and —

"Tsk."

I swallowed hard and tried to concentrate on the daydream instead of a sea of red X marks. I had the puck and the crowd was on its feet, cheering like crazy. I dodged around a second defender and had a clear shot at the crease. I lined up the puck and took the shot.

Score!

I smiled and opened my eyes, only to remember exactly where I was and exactly what was happening. How long did it take to grade a stupid test? I watched the second hand on the clock tick for several minutes, then stared out the window. What if I failed? I didn't want to think about it. What if —

"Mr. McDonald?" Mr. Holloway said.

"Yes?" I asked, scrambling to get up from my desk and walk toward him.

Every step brought me closer to knowing.

And I wasn't sure I wanted to know.

I stood at the edge of his desk, my hands sweating like crazy and my mouth totally dry.

"Seventy-six percent," Mr. Holloway said.

What? "Are you serious?" I gasped.

He didn't say anything, but lifted the paper so I could read the grade.

Whew! I actually did it!

"Next week's test will increase in difficulty. It's important that you be prepared."

"I will," I told him, and I meant it.

* * *

Mum and Dad were thrilled with my grade, but not thrilled enough to let me play that Saturday. Rules were rules, after all.

They took me to the rink so I could watch the game, and even though I knew I was stuck on the bench, I went to the locker room and put my gear on with the rest of the guys.

"I don't know how we're going to win this one," Patrick Chen said, shaking his head.

"You can do it," I told him, but the truth was, I wasn't so sure. With Bosko off at Math Provincials and me out of the game, who was going to play right wing?

I found out soon enough that Coach was putting Kenny in, which seemed totally nuts.

"Nugget, you know you're not playing," Coach said, when he saw me in uniform.

"I know," I told him. "I'm just here for support."

"Okay, as long as we understand each other."

"We do," I told him. I understood that I was going to have to sit there and watch my best pal try not to have a heart attack on the ice.

When the guys lined up to start the game, I crossed my fingers and hoped Kenny wouldn't freak out. After all, he'd never started before. I watched the ref drop the puck and we took possession right away. I stood up and cheered for my teammates.

It wasn't long before we took the lead, and even though I was surprised, Coach didn't seem to be. To my total shock and amazement, as the minutes passed, Kenny got some kind of a rhythm going with Patrick Chen and even scored during first period.

Patrick scored twice in the second, then Kenny added goal number four. Two goals for Kenny in one game!

"He's playing really well," Coach said.

"Yeah," I agreed, frowning.

I hated sitting there doing nothing and I was kind of jealous that Kenny was having such an awesome game. It stunk that the team was actually winning with no help from me.

Zero percent Nugget.

As the third period began, I wandered over to the snack bar for a bag of chips and a soggy hotdog. Compared to being out on the ice, the snack was a pretty crummy consolation prize.

Suddenly it seemed stupid to be all suited up with no chance of playing, so I headed back to the locker room to change. I thought I'd feel better in my jeans and sweatshirt, but it actually felt a bit worse, like I was just a fan and not a player. Like I wasn't even on the team anymore.

I joined Mum and Dad in the stands just as the game was ending. The second I sat down, my pal Kenny scored the final goal. We won the game. Well, *they* won the game, while I just watched.

I couldn't believe my benchwarming buddy had it in him, and I caught up with him after the game. I was determined not to be a jerk.

"Man, you were awesome," I told him.

Kenny grinned at me. "Thanks, Nugget. I guess today was my big chance."

"Yeah," I said, trying to sound enthusiastic. "Awesome."

I wished I hadn't even watched.

* * *

When Eddie Bosko showed up on my doorstep the following Monday, he had some horrible news. His Math team had won the provincial championship and they were going to Nationals in Toronto.

In two weeks.

"That's the weekend we play Shoreline!" I gasped.

"I know," he said, with a shrug. "But this is Nationals."

How were we supposed to have an undefeated season if we both wouldn't be able to play the number one team in the league?

"But Eddie —"

"Look, the guys won on Saturday, right?" he asked.

"Yeah, but it was a total fluke."

"That's not what I heard."

"Well, they weren't playing Shoreline, were they? We're doomed," I groaned, ready to give up.

Eddie shook his head. "Look, you have two more tests. If you make that seventy-five percent, you'll be back on the ice for the game."

"Yeah, right. If Coach actually lets me play those guys," I sighed.

"He'll let you play, Nugget. He needs you."

"You don't get it. I haven't grown any bigger and —"

"Get your dad to talk to him."

"What good will that do?"

"Maybe all Coach needs is for your dad to sign a waiver or something. You know, like if the Sharks break your legs, he won't sue the league or something."

"Break my legs? Is this supposed to be helping?"

"Hey, all I can do is make sure you have the Math part covered. So, are you ready to get down to business?" Eddie asked. "Geometry isn't exactly your strong point, so we need to get rolling."

While I did my best not to think about the oval ice rink, Eddie drilled me on a bunch of stupid triangles. After twenty minutes or so, when I was just starting to get warmed up, Wendy walked through the door. I stared at her for a second, feeling like there was something weird about her. Well, weirder than usual, anyway. I scanned her from head to toe, but other than a new jacket, I couldn't see anything different.

"What, Nugget?" she asked.

"Nothing . . . you just . . ." And that was when it hit me. She was *smiling*.

I glanced at Eddie, who looked totally stunned.

"That's my brother's jacket," he said, quietly.

"Yeah, it's Shane's," Wendy said, shrugging.

I couldn't help noticing her face was awfully pink.

"Why are you wearing it?" Eddie asked.

"He let me borrow it. I was cold in the car and —"

"He gave you a ride home?" Eddie almost choked.

"Duh," she said, walking toward the kitchen.

"From school?"

Wendy stopped again. "No, from McGinty's, if you must know."

"McGinty's restaurant?" Eddie's face was turning red and the whole situation was getting more awkward by the second.

I decided to steer us back to the reason he was there. "Why don't we get back to work here and —"

"McGinty's restaurant?" Eddie asked her again.

Oh, brother.

"What's your deal?" Wendy asked.

"Was it, like . . . a date?" Eddie barely got the words out.

Wendy rolled her eyes. "It was like a piece of lemon meringue pie and a hot chocolate."

I felt Eddie relax next to me. That is, until Wendy said, "The date's on Friday."

He stiffened up again and when Wendy walked into the kitchen, he just sat there.

"Ready?" I asked, anxious to move on to the real issue of mastering math and getting back on the ice.

"They're dating," he said, softly.

"I guess," I said, shrugging.

Eddie stared at his hands. "Shane and Wendy."

I didn't need a refresher. "Yeah. Your brother and my sister. Weird, eh?"

My tutor started slowly closing his books and loading them into his backpack.

"What are you doing?" I asked.

"I've got to go."

"What? Go where?" I asked. The test was only a few days away!

"I've just . . . I need to get out of here," he said, reaching for his pens and pencils.

"But we just started and —"

"I'll see you tomorrow." And with that, Eddie Bosko walked out the front door.

What was I supposed to do? I stared at the textbook.

I only had four stinkin' days!

"Your pet gorilla left?" Wendy asked, coming out of the kitchen with a glass of milk.

"Yeah, thanks to you."

"Me?"

"Yes, you." I knew it wasn't her fault, but I had to blame someone.

"I didn't do anything," Wendy snapped.

"You went out with his brother."

"So?"

"So, he's in love with you!"

"That kid? Your tutor?" She laughed.

"Yeah."

"Nugget, he's eleven."

"Almost twelve."

"And Shane is *seventeen*. He can drive, for crying out loud."

"I know, but —"

She shook her head. "Why would that kid be in love with me?"

"I don't know, Wendy. You're asking the wrong guy. Geez, you're my sister, and even if you weren't, I don't want anything to do with girls."

"In love with me, eh? Interesting," she said, starting to climb the stairs.

"Just be nice to him when he comes over, okay?" That is, if he ever walked through the door again. "I can't pass Math without him."

I doubted she was even listening.

The next day, Eddie suggested we study in the library for a change, and that was totally cool with me. The less he was around my sister, the better my chances of passing.

* * *

That night, Dad made popcorn to snack on while we watched the Canucks smoke Anaheim, but I told him I had to study for my Math test instead.

"Good decision," Dad said, filling a small bowl I could take to my room. "I'm going to miss watching with you, but you're making the right choice."

The right choice? When I heard him cheering at the television, I found that hard to believe. When I struggled through four pages of Math questions, I doubted it even more. And when I took the test that Friday?

Well, that was the worst moment of the week.

I struggled all the way through, and second-guessed almost every answer. I went through half of an eraser in the first two pages! When I started freaking out, I sat back in my chair and closed my eyes for a few seconds, remembering the two hours I'd spent in the library with Eddie Bosko, just twenty-four hours earlier.

I'd left that study session feeling like I had a handle on Geometry, but guessed I was wrong.

I was totally lost.

With my eyes still closed, I pictured Eddie's face across from me at the table, encouraging me.

I opened my eyes to keep going and after what seemed like only three minutes, Mr. Holloway told me, "Time is up, Mr. McDonald."

"I just have one question left."

"Time is up." He collected my paper and I stayed at my desk to wait again.

This time, I was prepared. I'd brought a book to read, called *Watching Carter*. It was written by the same author as *Over the Moon*, and it was really good, but not quite good enough to keep me from worrying about my test score. I read a whole chapter while I waited, and when I was done, I had no idea what I'd read.

So I started to read it again.

About halfway through, Mr. Holloway called me up to his desk. It was worse than the last time and I actually felt sick to my stomach.

"Unfortunate news," Mr. Holloway said, holding the paper up for me to see.

I only got a seventy-one.

Nuts!

"That brings your average down to seventy-three and a half percent."

Would he round up to seventy-four? I doubted it. "That means I have to get —"

"*Seventy-eight* on the final test."

Double, triple and quadruple nuts!

"Seventy-eight," I repeated, because I didn't know what else to say.

I was going to have to study even harder, as if that were possible.

Chapter Sixteen

The next day, I sat in the stands with my family to watch the game against Comox. They'd always been a pretty good team and I knew it would be a close game. I wished, for the millionth time, that Math hadn't gotten me into this mess. Why hadn't I just done the stupid homework assignments all along?

Because I never thought I'd be stuck on the stands if I didn't.

I watched my teammates warm up by skating laps and passing the puck back and forth. I wished my own warm-up wasn't a hot chocolate, since whipped cream was a pretty lame substitute for scoring goals.

The ref blew his whistle and once the guys were lined up, the game got started.

Patrick took possession and started hustling toward the visitors' net. He had one guy right on his tail and he passed the puck at the perfect moment, which was right before he tripped over his skates and wiped out.

At least the pass had been clean. My parents and I

jumped up to cheer as Eddie Bosko slipped the puck between a defenseman's skates and picked it up again on the other side.

"That kid is great," Dad said.

Great? "Well, *good*, anyway . . ." I said, but he wasn't listening.

Just then, Bosko got checked and lost the puck. We all groaned, but within seconds he'd snatched it back and we were cheering again. I wasn't quite as loud as everyone else, especially when he scored what could have been my goal.

Man, it was hard to watch someone else do my job.

Or *our* job.

"So, Math and hockey are covered," Dad said. "What else can this kid do?"

I hated to think.

As I watched the game, I thought about all the things I could have done differently, and how much better they could have turned out. I made some mistakes in Math class, but even worse was the way I'd hoped for Bosko's failure and didn't even root for Kenny when he finally got his chance to be a star.

Pretty lame, really.

At least I'd have a chance to make up for it, though. If I got my seventy-eight on the final Math test, I'd be back on the ice in time to play Victoria. Eddie Bosko and I would tear the ice up . . . together.

And there was always the possibility that Coach would give in and let me play against Shoreline before then.

A guy could hope, anyway.

I got more excited about the game as I watched Jason make a killer save, then Patrick score a goal. I was proud to be part of such a good team, and even more proud when we won.

I even cheered when Eddie scored the winning goal, and only felt the tiniest bit jealous.

* * *

During the week before the Shoreline game and Math-geek Nationals, Eddie and I worked on word problems in the library every single afternoon.

"How do you feel about the test?" he asked.

"Nervous."

"Don't be. You're better than you think you are."

"Really?" I asked, seriously doubting it.

"Dude, we've been practisng pretty hard. You've spent more time on Math in the past month than I bet you did in your whole life."

"That's true."

"You can totally do it, Nugget."

"I hope so," I said, starting to read over the next problem.

Eddie cleared his throat. "So, did Wendy say anything about her date with my brother?"

"Not really. We don't talk about that kind of stuff."

"Sure," he said, nodding. "No big deal. I was just wondering if they were, you know . . . going out again."

As hard as it was to believe, it seemed like it was my turn to help Bosko. "You know, she's a lot older than you."

"Not that much."

"She's sixteen, Bosko." I tried to think of the best way to say what I knew was true. "I don't think she'll ever want to hang out with someone her little brother's age. You can't take it personally."

"That's cool," he said, even though I could tell he didn't feel that way. He turned to his book.

That was when I remembered something I'd noticed in Math class. "Besides, I don't know why you'd care about

Wendy when Carrie Tanaka is always looking at you."

Eddie stared at me. "She is?"

"Yeah. I think she likes you."

I would have been grossed out if anyone had said that to me, about any of the girls at school, but Eddie Bosko started to smile.

"Carrie Tanaka? Are you serious?" he asked.

I nodded. "Check it out next time we're in Mr. Holloway's class."

"Cool," he said, his face turning a bit red. "Thanks, Nugget." He cleared his throat again. "I guess we should get rolling on these problems."

I nodded, relieved that we could talk about something else.

Girl problems were a serious pain in the butt.

* * *

That final Friday test turned out to be totally brutal. I knew my hockey season was in danger as soon as I read the first question, and doomed by the time I reached the third one.

But I did my best.

When I finally finished with the test and was sure my head was about to explode from the effort, I had to sit and wait for the stupid results again. I had a book with me, but I didn't feel like reading. In fact, I didn't feel like doing anything but stare out the window.

The marking took longer than usual, and when Mr. Holloway told me he was finished, I figured I was too.

I walked up to his desk, my hands balled into fists as I waited for the bad news.

"Mr. McDonald, how do you think it went?"

"I dunno," I mumbled. Seventy-eight percent was way too much to hope for.

I'd blown it for sure.

"I beg your pardon?" Mr. Holloway asked. "And please make eye contact when you speak, Mr. McDonald."

I looked right at him. "I'm not sure how it went, Mr. Holloway."

"Did you read through all of the questions first?"

"Yes."

"Did you take your time?"

"Yes."

"Review your work?"

"Yes."

"So there you have it."

Huh?

He must have seen how confused I was. "Now you know how to tackle a test." He paused for a second, then smiled. "And even better? Now you know how to pass it."

"Seriously?" I asked.

"Eighty-one percent."

"No way!"

"Excellent job, Mr. McDonald. Truly excellent."

Excellent! I couldn't believe it. I'd never come close to a mark that awesome in Math!

"Three tests and three solid grades. I can't say that I'm an expert when it comes to the vernacular for our nation's sport, but —"

"Vernacu-what?"

"Terminology," Mr. Holloway explained, but that didn't actually explain anything.

"I don't know what that —"

"What I am attempting to get across, Mr. McDonald, is that while I haven't mastered the language of hockey, I am quite certain that you have just achieved the mathematics equivalent of a hat trick."

It took me a second or two to get it.

A hat trick? In Math? It was incredible! And if that wasn't amazing enough, something happened a second later that I *really* couldn't believe.

Mr. Holloway gave me a high five.

Chapter Seventeen

When I shared my Math score, Mum and Dad hugged me and told me how proud they were. It felt awesome, especially because I'd never imagined how cool good grades could be.

At the dinner table that night, I told Dad how important the Shoreline game was to me, especially since I'd been missing out on playing already. He and Mum both listened to what I had to say about Bosko being away that weekend and even Wendy managed to stay quiet while I explained why I needed to help the Cougars beat Shoreline.

When I was finished, Mum agreed that Dad could talk to Coach O'Neal and give their permission for me to play.

Considering I'd convinced my parents that it was a good idea, I was totally shocked when Dad told me the next day that Coach had disagreed.

It was totally unfair and I didn't know what to do, so I stopped by Coach's office to talk to him myself.

He sat at a desk covered with pictures of Cougars teams through the years. There were framed news clippings from when the team won big games up on the walls, and he had a trophy shelf with awards and a couple of photos from back in the days when he played. Coach O'Neal made it to the minors, but not the NHL.

"I don't have to ask why you're here," he said.

"The Shoreline game," I said, nodding. "Bosko is going to be out of town and —"

"Nugget, we've been through this before," he said.

"I know I'm small, Coach, but I'm tough and —"

"They're huge."

"I know, but —"

"Your Dad and I discussed this already and he understands my concern."

I felt my hands ball into fists. It wasn't fair. "I can't do anything about my size, Coach."

"I don't know what to tell you. I wouldn't feel good about letting you go out there. If you hurt yourself —"

"I've been hurt before," I reminded him. "Lots of times."

"I just don't feel right about it."

"But —"

He stopped me by holding up one hand. "I'm the coach, and my decision is final."

I couldn't think of anything to say, so I just stared at him.

"I'm sorry, Nugget. Maybe next year."

"Maybe," I sighed, and started to leave.

"Listen, I'm going to need you in every other game this season. I hope I can count on you."

"You can," I told him.

On the way home, I tried to understand how it was possible that after all of my hard work on the ice, off the ice, in Math class, at the dining room table and everywhere else, I *still* didn't get to play.

It totally stunk.

What didn't stink was that we ended up beating Shoreline.

Kenny broke the tie in the last seconds of the game and the crowd went totally crazy. He looked so shocked and happy when the guys swarmed him, patting his back and helmet, I couldn't stop smiling. But even though I was super proud of him, I had to admit that I wished it was me. I hoped with everything I had that next year I'd be out there playing Shoreline.

In the meantime, I knew I'd be a part of the next game and every game after that. After all, the season had barely started, and Coach said needed me. We'd be taking on Victoria the very next Saturday, and we'd play a team from Nanaimo the week after that.

Sure, I regretted missing out on Shoreline, but I had plenty to look forward to.

Starting with the Canucks game and that perfect shot from centre ice.

* * *

For the next week, I practised shooting in the driveway every night after I did my homework. I had to be ready for my big moment. I spent every spare second imagining myself at centre ice, calm, cool and totally ready to amaze the crowd with one big, bad blast of the puck.

Everyone at school knew I was going to be taking the shot, and every day more kids wished me luck. When I went grocery shopping with Mum, the cashier wished me luck. Mr. Howard, our next door neighbour, told me he'd be rooting for me and wished me luck.

Luck, luck, luck.

The truth was, I didn't need any. It was all about practise, and I'd done so much of that, I knew had nothing to worry about. Shooting was as natural to me as breathing and it felt like my whole life had been building toward that moment in Rogers Arena.

I couldn't wait.

* * *

When Dad and I got up on the morning of the Canucks game, I was shocked that I'd actually slept. I'd laid out my clothes the night before, so I was totally ready to go. Once I was out of the shower, I put on my favourite jeans, a pair of Vans, a blue hoodie and my Jean Ducette jersey on top of it.

I looked like a super fan.

No, I looked like the ultimate fan.

No, it was more —

"Like a bride on her wedding day," Wendy said, when she saw me standing in front of the mirror.

"Very funny," I told her.

"Nugget?" she said.

"Yeah?"

Before I had a chance to defend myself, my sister was *hugging* me. "Good luck," she whispered.

I started to say I didn't need any, but knew that wasn't the point. After all, Wendy didn't even hug me on Christmas. "Thanks," I told her, and meant it.

"Ready?" Dad asked, when I got to the kitchen.

"Definitely," I told him. I looked for a bag lunch on the counter top, and when I didn't see anything, I turned to Mum.

"You guys are going to have a great time," she said, pulling me into my second hug of the day. "And if that means greasy hamburgers and too much pop, I don't want the details. Deal?"

"Deal," I told her.

"Have a wonderful day, Jonathan," she told me. "And good luck."

Dad and I drove to Nanaimo, where we could catch the ferry to the mainland, and when we got there the lineup was massive.

"You've got to love weekend traffic," Dad sighed. When he paid, he asked which sailing we'd be on.

"Maybe the ten," the lady said. "For sure the eleven."

We pulled into row twelve and sat in the car. Dad had a newspaper to read, and he let me have the comics. None of them were very funny, but at least reading them killed some time.

My very first NHL game. The day had finally come!

We missed the ten o'clock sailing by about fifteen cars, so Dad sent me to the concession to get a coffee for him and a juice for myself. I must have checked my watch a thousand times while we waited for the next ferry.

When we finally boarded, Dad and I went straight to the cafeteria for eggs and stuff, but they were already serving lunch. That meant I got to have a Legendary Burger, fries with gravy and a Coke for breakfast.

Awesome!

When we pulled out of the terminal to start the trip, the captain honked the horn a couple of times, and the kids on the deck outside covered their ears and cried like babies. Dad and I found seats at the front, and he gave me a few quarters to play video games. I couldn't concentrate, so I wandered around the decks for a little while, then went to the gift shop to check out their hockey books for inspiration. (Not that I needed any.)

I was ready to score.

* * *

After an hour and a half on the water, we pulled into Horseshoe Bay. The lineup waiting to go back to the island was even bigger than the one we'd been in that morning.

Geez. Why didn't they just build a bridge?

We drove up onto the highway and I sat back in my seat, daydreaming about the game.

"Excited?" Dad asked.

"Totally."

"A little nervous, too?"

"Nope."

"Really?"

"I'm ready for this."

"If you say so," he said, smiling.

"It's not like I'll be trying to solve a Math problem in front of thousands of people."

"Which you could do now, thanks to hard work and Eddie Bosko."

"That's not really the point, Dad."

"True," he said. "But I know I'd be nervous about this shot."

"I'm not," I told him, but the nerves kicked in when we parked at the stadium and I saw just how huge it was. There would be a lot of people watching.

Dad and I walked to the main gate, along with hundreds of fans. Everywhere I looked, I saw Canucks shirts, jackets and hats. I even saw a guy with the team logo painted on his face!

When we got inside, I couldn't believe how loud it was. They had stalls set up for selling Canucks gear, and stands for beer and food. I had a little bit of money with me, so I bought a program.

Jean Ducette was on the cover, and I was about to see him, live!

It was way too awesome.

"I'm gonna frame this," I told Dad.

"A nice addition to your room," he said, patting my back.

All of a sudden I heard a bunch of noise behind us, and it seemed like the whole crowd was booing at once. When I turned to look, there was a guy wearing a Flames jersey, waving at everybody. The crowd booed even louder.

"We're gonna cream you," he shouted over the racket.

Without even thinking, I started booing too. He deserved it!

Dad and I found our entry and when we walked through the doorway, my mouth dropped open like a flounder.

The place was gigantic! The biggest TV screen I'd ever seen was hanging above the rink, flashing highlights from the past few games. The ceiling looked like it was too high for oxygen, but there were people sitting all the way in the top row. The rink probably looked like a cake from way up there, with players for sprinkles!

Dad checked the tickets and we started down the stairs toward the ice. We were already close, but we kept getting closer. When we reached our seats, we were right at the centre line, only six rows from the ice.

"Nice job on the tickets," Dad said, pointing at the seats.

Holy smokes. We were practically *on* the ice.

And even better? I actually would be!

* * *

The game was everything I dreamed it would be (except when some lady sang "O Canada" like it was opera or something and I had to cover my ears).

The crowd went crazy when each of the players was introduced.

I couldn't believe I was that close to Jean Ducette!

There was so much to see, I couldn't keep track of it all.

I stared at the players when they warmed up.

I bit my lip when they got into position.

Even the refs looked cool!

I shouted with everyone else when the puck was dropped and I didn't stop shouting for the whole first period. The seat was pointless, because I was on my feet the whole time, too.

Jean Ducette was incredible, and soon we were winning, 2–0.

Totally awesome.

Halfway through the second period, a woman tapped me on the shoulder.

"Jonathan McDonald?"

"Yes," I nodded.

"I'm Katie, with the Canucks promotional team. Are you ready to come with me?"

I nodded again and when I stood up, Dad gave me a big hug and ruffled my hair, like I wasn't about to be on the big screen!

I followed Katie up the stairs, patting my hair back down and starting to feel even more nervous.

The crowd was gigantic, and so loud! I pretended they were cheering for me. We waited for the period to end and I couldn't hear anything the announcer said, until my name blasted over the speakers.

"Go ahead, Jonathan," Katie said.

I stepped onto the green carpet path they'd rolled out to centre ice. A grey-haired man in a suit shook my hand and let me say hi into the microphone.

"Are you ready?" he asked.

All I could do was nod.

He handed me a stick and I carried it with me to the very edge of the carpet.

It was my moment!

I lined myself up with the goal.

I'd been practising that *exact* shot for a month solid.

I was shaking a little, but I knew it was going to be easy peasy.

The crowd cheered for me, and for a second, I almost felt like a real pro.

I lifted the stick.

I was all set up for a perfect shot.

I took a deep breath.

And swung.

I hit that puck harder than ever before.

I watched it zoom toward the net.

Then veer to the left.

Uh-oh.

My whole body tensed.

Just a little more to the right.

To the right.

No, the *right*!

I almost screamed like a girl when it slid right past my wide open target.

I missed!

I missed?

The crowd groaned and I felt my face burning.

What just happened?

"Sorry, Jonathan," the grey-haired man said.

And just like that, the biggest moment of my life was over.

I missed.

He told the crowd to give me a hand, but I was in shock.

How could I have missed?

He passed me an envelope and I walked back down the green carpet, unable to look at anyone. It was hard to put one foot in front of the other to get back to the stands and all I wanted to do was disappear. How was I supposed to face my teammates or the rest of the kids at school?

I'd totally blown it!

I shuffled along the carpet and when I got to the end and was ready to step off the ice, a huge Canucks uniform appeared directly in front of me, blocking the way.

When I looked up, it was Jean Ducette.

My hero.

Nuts!

He'd seen my rotten shot!

Could the day get any worse?

"You surprised me," he said, in a deep voice.

"Me too," I told him, glumly.

"For a small one, you have a lot of power, no?"

"What?" I asked, thinking I'd heard him wrong.

"Your speed with the puck," he said, patting me on the back. "It is serious."

"It is?"

"Impressive," he told me.

What? Jean Ducette was impressed by me? I couldn't even speak.

"Want me to sign your jersey?"

"Are you kidding?" I asked.

"No," he laughed, as the grey-haired man handed him a pen. "Your name?"

"Nugget," I said, without thinking.

Jean Ducette looked confused. He turned to the man and asked. "Qu'est-ce que c'est?"

The man put his fingers close together to show something small. "Pepite."

Jean Ducette laughed and ruffled my hair, just like Dad had done. "Pepite. I like it."

And just like that, I did too.

Maybe it was because my number one hero was saying it, but Nugget sounded way cooler in French!

Pepite.

That was *me*.

I turned around and grinned as the legendary Jean Ducette signed the back of my jersey.

When he was done, I turned to face him. "I just wish I hadn't missed," I told him.

"Everybody misses sometimes," he said. "If we always scored and always won, it wouldn't be . . . interesting."

I'd never thought of it like that. "I guess not," I told him.

He patted me on the back. "You will get bigger, better and stronger, Pepite. This is only the beginning for you."

I thanked him and practically floated back to my seat.

When I got there, Dad looked sad, like someone had died. "I'm sorry Jonathan. I can imagine how disappointed you are."

I thought about what my hero had said to me. "It's okay, Dad."

"What?" he asked, eyebrows raised in surprise.

I shrugged, pretty sure Jean Ducette wasn't just talking about hockey. "Sometimes I'm going to score and sometimes I'm going to miss. That's what keeps it . . . interesting."

Dad was quiet for a minute. "I'm impressed," he finally said.

It was the second time I'd heard that in a few minutes, and it felt good.

I liked impressing people.

"So what's in the envelope?" he asked.

"I don't know," I said, ripping it open. Inside was a gift certificate for Pro-Sports. For $200!

First Jean Ducette, now this?

I had to be the luckiest kid on the planet.

Sure, I was sharing my position with Bosko and I had a long way to go with Math. I'd missed playing in three Cougars games *and* the shot of a lifetime in front of thousands of people.

But somehow everything had turned out okay. Way better than okay, actually.

I looked around the stadium, at all the fans who were there for my first NHL game, and it felt awesome.

Dad's eyes widened when he looked at the gift certificate. "Whoa! That's enough for the helmet you wanted, isn't it?"

I smiled and nodded, too happy for words.

About the Author
W.C. Mack was born in Vancouver., B.C. and now lives in Portland, Oregon. Always a Canucks fan, W.C. Mack has also been known to cheer for the Portland Winterhawks.

Acknowledgments
Many thanks to my editor, Diane Kerner, who pointed me toward the rink, and to my agent, Sally Harding, who encouraged me to go for it (even though it wasn't rugby).